TO LIVE AND DIE IN DEEP DEUCE

TO LIVE AND DIE IN DEEP DEUCE

A Lou Nayland Novel

by Scott R. Hartshorn

LeVel
BEST BOOKS

Historia

First published by Level Best Books/Historia 2020

This novel is entirely a work of fiction. The names, characters and incidents portrayed in it are the work of the author's imagination. Any resemblance to actual persons, living or dead, events or localities is entirely coincidental.

Scott R. Hartshorn asserts the moral right to be identified as the author of this work.

Second edition

ISBN: 978-1-953789-11-2

Cover art by Level Best Designs

This book was professionally typeset on Reedsy.
Find out more at reedsy.com

To my Wife Anne

Contents

Praise for TO LIVE AND DIE IN DEEP DEUCE

"A fascinating blend of mystery, historical fiction, and family saga. Compelling characters intertwined in an intriguing storyline bring the 1930s Oklahoma City to life. You can almost hear the smooth jazz, see a city in between cow-town, oil boom, and modernity, and feel the heat of the warm days and hot nights. A story that will leave you wanting more."—Jeannie Pappas

"Hartshorn brings us back to the classical Noir thriller replete with a large and varied cast of eccentrics and villains. Set in historical Oklahoma City, readers will find themselves transported to a city trying to grow beyond the cattle and cowboys it was known for."—Justin Olmstead, Ph.D.

"Harken back to the steamy, sexy world of pulp fiction novels and film noir cinema. The novel weaves a scandalous tale of jazz, voyeurism, adultery and murder in the noir of the 1930s."—Professor Michelle Brockmeir

Chapter One

That Friday night, the heat rolled off the prairie. The Great Depression, red dust, and oil, characterized the Big Friendly in July of 1935. The Indians' pennant race in the Texas League, as well as the wild new sound of Charles Christian's Jazz explosion, held the city under their spells. On this sizzling, steamy evening, the Friday workforce in the big little cow town hoped the sun would fall faster in the orange western sky. They wanted relief, and twilight wasn't coming soon enough.

The collaborated sound of jazz was the very thing the swell-looking canary in the stretch Packard Twelve breezer was heading to enjoy this evening. She expertly maneuvered the roadster into the narrow parking space on North Central Avenue. Lauren Camp was lean and rangy, with a well-formed mouth and dimpled chin. Her highly defined legs were covered in the sheerest of silk stockings, the display of which Will H. Hays wouldn't have approved of. She carefully removed her felt tilt hat, placed it on the seat of the car and slowly smoothed the wrinkles from her glad rags. Lauren checked her makeup in the golden-framed vanity mirror she took from her Joseff of Hollywood satin purse and removed her wedding band, placing it in her purse. Her platinum bobbed hair was parted in the middle and looked slightly askew, and she smoothed back the strays with a carefully manicured hand. Even though she was born and raised in the Southwest, her appearance and demeanor spoke of a pampered woman from the Upper East Side. As she walked along Second Avenue towards the Aldridge Theatre, she was aware that she was far from her side of town, but she was no stranger to the power created by the jazz and blues joints of Deep Deuce, widely known

1

as the "Harlem of the South."

The Deuce was the thriving center of the segregated neighborhood created by the exclusively white city council to discourage integration. The council, along with Lawrence Wadsworth Davis's financial and political backing, in an attempt to confine the city's black families, had set aside a dozen blocks around Second Street and eastward, now known as "Deep Deuce."

Since its creation, the Deep Deuce had developed into a thriving business community occupied by retail shops and services owners like doctors and lawyers. It bragged of a flourishing entertainment district with establishments like the Aldridge Theatre, a movie house most of the week that served as a performing arts venue on the weekends. New Harlem's most popular music venues included the Aldridge Theatre, Slaughter's Hall, and Ruby's Dance and Grill. All provided the colored community and daring white outsiders an opportunity to enjoy watered-down drinks and jazz in anonymity.

Two men dressed in the most brightly colored shark skin suits, with the taller one wearing a yellow carination in his lapel, took a double take as they walked by the bold and confident white woman who appeared not to give a damn about what the locals thought. Lauren returned a feline smile back in their direction, acknowledging their stares as she proceeded to the Aldridge to catch the first set of the Oklahoma City Blue Devils, a dynamic jazz group with an extraordinary spirit, legendary talent and a wild and reckless playing style.

Lauren paused as she looked at the musicians' placards hanging on each side of the chrome front doors of the Art Deco theater. Onlookers would naturally assume she was checking her makeup in the reflection of the glass. However, a careful observer would have discerned her scanning the list of bands playing that evening. The bobbed-blonde only dropped in on the Aldridge on the nights that Lesley "Sticks" Timons performed on the drums.

She stood reading the posters before turning and looking over at the hotel that sat across the street from the Aldridge. The Littlepage, a small, moderately priced, two-story red brick hotel containing storefronts that faced 2nd Street and Central Avenue. The hotel consisted of twenty-five rooms located on the second floor. A brightly colored wood door, facing Central, was situated between the storefronts on the first floor.

The street bustled with folks going about their daily business. As she casually looked next door to Hayward's Billiards Hall, four colored gentlemen came out of the double swinging screen doors and briefly stopped to stare curiously in her direction. One of them said something to the others, whereupon they laughed and walked east towards Robinson's Drug store.

Lauren scrutinized a small group of colored women exiting Louis's Grocery and Market. A heavy woman bulging from her pregnancy led the pack while four small children darted in and out of her skirts. They all gazed at Lauren with amusement as she stood before the Aldridge.

The gorgeous blonde ignored all their glances. She couldn't care less what other people thought. Smiling to herself, she reflected on the many lust-filled evenings she had spent in the Littlepage. These women would never understand or appreciate the encounters that occurred on the second floor in a tiny little hotel room. That was his room, the man she shared her trysts with, who right now was warming up inside the Aldridge. She hoped her drummer played well tonight. It made him more passionate and loving. His sexuality elevated her passion with the man she both desired and despised.

Lauren snapped back to reality, opened the smoked glass door, and entered the poorly lit auditorium. The club doorman, a large dark man with a shaved head, appeared from his small fox-den of an office, set off to the right of the theater's entrance. For a big man, he possessed a whisper of a voice. When he spoke, it always reminded the woman of a shy teenage girl.

She spoke to the hulk of a man. "Evening, George."

"Good evening, ma'am," the large doorman politely greeted her. "You're early tonight. The guys are just setting up."

Slowly, her eyes adjusted to the dim light. The Aldridge only had few customers, but she knew it was early. She looked back up at the mountain of a doorman.

"Hope the crowd's hopping tonight."

He gave her a shake of his large head. "Me too, ma'am."

She scanned the room. "I think I'll get a drink and listen to them rehearse.

You're looking good tonight, George," Lauren said with a wink as she strolled away from the bouncer toward the rolling bar along the back wall.

George watched, noticing the navy blue dress she wore, narrow in the right places, full in the others. He watched her muscles tighten and relax under her fitted skirt as she covered the distance to the bar. He thought to himself, *I need a walk in the rain every time that woman comes in. Old Sticks has himself something there.*

Several musicians on the risers started tuning up their trumpets, licorice sticks, tubs, and a lone dog house the band used in its sessions. The group seemed to be arguing about the sequence of tunes for the night's sets.

Near the back of the rise, "Sticks" Timons sat behind his drums. Even in the dim light of the club, Lauren could make-out Lesley in his tailored black suit, ivory shirt and shimmering blue tie. Lesley Timons possessed the skin color of dark coffee. His wide muscular shoulders and broad chest narrowed at his waist like the top heavyweight contender, Joe Louis. Even though only six foot two, he had the appearance of being taller. He had curly black hair with pencil-thin eyebrows that did not quite meet over his thin nose. His dark brown eyes had a shine close to tears. A forgotten unlit cigar was clamped in his mouth. He needed a shave. He always needed a shave. This was the man who drew the uptown woman into the Aldridge.

Lauren enjoyed Timons' company, but knew little about him other than he had been born in Grove, in 1905, when Oklahoma was still Indian Territory and that he had been raised by his maternal grandmother. She was also well aware of his reputation as a charming rogue.

Timons' musical talents had grown out of his grandmother's evangelical church and black gospel. The old men of the neighborhood passed time with their music. They taught him to play guitar and drums. He once told her he had been a bass drummer in high school. After graduating from Seneca High School, he attended Kansas University where he studied sax, violin, piano, drums, voice, composition, and arranging. Shortly thereafter, he played with Bennie Moten for a while before joining the Blue Devils.

The Deb continued over to the bar. Behind it stood a handsome young woman wiping the red oak with a soggy towel. Cecelia May gave the rangy blonde a catbird smile. Lauren observed that Cecelia was too tall to be cute, but had a minxy look that most men would find alluring.

Cecelia's eyes flicked from the woman's shoulders to her waist and up again to her platinum blond hair with a disapproving stare.

"I'll have a sidecar, with a lemon twist, and none of that barleycorn, use the cognac on the left end of the rack."

Cecelia let out a huff as she made the drink quickly and pushed the sweating glass towards the woman. "You're gonna cause trouble in here tonight. Why don't you just leave after you've had your drink? I'll even buy it if you walk out now."

The saucy blonde smiled her best toothy grin while putting a Lincoln on the bar. "Keep the change," she remarked as she turned and walked over to an empty table on the far side of the stage.

Lauren sipped her sweet drink while fixing her steel-blue eyes on Timons. She thought he looked good tonight.

Lesley felt her presence, looked up, winked in her direction, and returned to his music. The other members of the band began to take their positions on stage. Lauren recognized most of them. She was not a regular, but she was here enough to know their names. The most recognizable in the group was Edward Christian, bandleader and younger brother of the great swing and jazz guitarist Charles Christian. The members of the band dressed identically, in black suits and white shirts, but each wore a different colored tie.

The Aldridge slowly filled. More couples entered, ordered drinks and sat at the pine wood tables. The center of the room remained open for dancing. Moments later Jim Dodson looked down on his guitar as his fingers touched the strings soundlessly, he then strummed a chord or two over the round sounding hole and threw back his head and began to play "Squabblin," a three minute riff of the band's own composition and a hometown crowd's favorites. The hoofers and cement mixers moved out onto the dance floor and began to twist and turn to the beat.

Lauren stayed at her table, enjoying the rhythm of jazz. The beat of the music reached into her chest and took hold of her heart. She felt the internal pounding as the energy of the drums raced through her limbs. Her skin began to tingle and her breath became short with anticipation.

The band played a twenty minute set and broke. Timons, the last off the stage, walked to the bar. He ordered bourbon over ice, picked up his drink, and worked his way around the room, greeting guests and friends. He avoided the blonde's table, but casually looked her way. Lauren watched him work the room. Her heart race slightly.

Lauren had slept with Lesley a dozen times. But she felt no emotion akin to love for him. Her needs were different. Timons was a sexual obsession she hadn't been able to shake since their first encounter. Even though she loved and adored her husband, she still needed to be fulfilled by the man currently working the room toward her.

Lauren reflected on the cause of this addiction, one that consumed her every waking hour. She was fully aware that her entanglement with the drummer wasn't only morally wrong because she was married, but legally wrong as well, because, in Oklahoma, it was a crime to be with a man of color. Hell, Lauren thought, those crumbs in the State Capital had even put a name to it, "miscegenation," and it carried a five year prison term.

Timons suddenly sat at her table and asked, "You here to appreciate my music tonight or do you have time to star watch when I'm done?"

Lauren smiled and whispered, "The team has a three day stand in Tulsa, so I'm lonely."

He smirked. "So star watching it is." He got up and went back to the stage behind his tubs set.

Lauren walked over to the scowling Cecelia and ordered another drink. The band played six more sets. Lauren sipped her drink. The band finally finished close to midnight, and though it had been a Ring-a-Ding-Ding night, the place soon cleared out, except for the cleaning staff and Cecelia putting away the liquor. Timons put his coat on, picked up his last bourbon and walked over to Lauren.

"Time for us to go see the stars, Angel."

Cecelia watched them leave together and shook her head in disgust as the couple walked out the front door into the hot, humid July night.

6

Chapter Two

Outside on 2nd Street the couple watched the drunks from Ruby's Bar and Grill weave along the pavement, unwilling to give up the night and face the approaching sunrise. Some had female companions to assure them that fun still lay ahead. Lesley recognized one of the women, a local songbird named Myra, a good-looking brunette when seen from a distance. But she lost ground when you got close. She was dressed in her usual flashy clothes that carried bargain basement labels you can't tear off. Her dress lacked any shoulder straps and appeared to be falling off and be halfway gone. Her companions, those kinds of women you never see during daylight hours and always appear road worn when you do, carried on laughing and stumbling along with their dates around the corner as Lauren and Timons watched their performance.

The pair took all this in as they stood a moment looking up and down the street. Hundreds of cicadas hummed in the distance. Smoothly Timons grasped her hand, squeezing it firmly as they continued on towards the Littlepage Hotel. The locusts continued to beat their wings in the darkness.

A lone light shone from the lobby of the Littlepage through the front window as the couple approached. The glow allowed the couple to see the night clerk asleep at his post.

Lesley opened the door, allowing Lauren to enter, her elegant scent filling his nose. He followed her inside and walked across the polished hardwood floors to the desk clerk. Lauren remained patiently next to the lobby's lone coffee table and two straight-back chairs. Looking down, she observed the magazines spread upon the table. Her eye caught *The Negro Motorist Green*

Book. She picked it up and flipped through the pages.

Thomas, the night shift manager, slept with his feet crossed upon a desk with a copy of the *Black Dispatch* spread over his chest. Timons read the front page upside down. *Professor F.D. Moor provides a profound and electrifying address to 50 new Degree recipients at Langston University.* As Lesley read, Thomas continued to saw away in his padded swivel chair with the contentment of the old. He snored with a slow whistle with each exhale of his breath. Timons tapped lightly on the chrome night bell. Thomas startled, and through sleepy eyes, looked up and put his feet down on the freshly polished tiled floor.

"Evening, Sticks," the night clerk uttered.

"Can I have my room key, Thomas?" Lesley inquired.

"Sure. You have a good set tonight, brother?" Thomas asked.

"Yes, but the night's still young," he said, winking.

The clerk stood up and turned to the twenty or so wooden mail and key slots, reached into box number twenty-five, removed the skeleton key from a brass hook and handed it to Timons. "It must be nice to be young and have all that energy," he joked.

Timons took the key and walked to the base of the stairs, putting his arm around his blonde companion. Lauren grabbed the iron railing with her right hand, and with some intention, placed her Delman covered toes on the first red carpeted step and proceeded slowly up the staircase, knowing she had an audience. The pair proceeded up the narrow stairs as the night clerk watched them, or more precisely watched Lauren walk up the stairs. As she climbed, her ass muscles clung to the thin material of her skirt giving the appearance of the shoulder muscles of a large predator cat on the prowl. With each step she took, Thomas thought to himself, *I need to walk around in the rain every time I see that dame.*

The couple hit the top of the staircase in unison directly across from room 25. The woman took the man's drink from his right hand as he inserted the key into the lock and turned. The lock bolt clicked open; Lesley turned the knob. The couple entered. Silence and darkness filled the room. Nothing stirred, inside or out, but the dull hum of the cicadas rising and falling outside the open window.

Once inside the only light came from the glow of the neon sign atop the Aldridge marquee. Even with the windows open, no wind blew into the room and the night remained hot and sticky. From outside, the cicadas beating wings sounded mournful in the dry summer trees, creating an eerie feeling for the couple. The atmosphere fit the moment.

Lesley didn't want to change the ambience of the room, so he left the bedside light off, but pulled down the bead chain causing the brass-bladed ceiling fan to begin a slow whirl. The slow-turning ceiling fan was the only form of cooling in the room. He walked over to a well-worn, scuffed dresser and removed a bottle of Old Grand-Dad from the top drawer and poured three fingers worth into two whiskey tumblers and then added tap water to the woman's drink from the white porcelain sink.

Lauren plucked at the collar of her chiffon blouse. A flowered Saks Fifth Avenue bra and chemise showed beneath it. Removing her skirt revealed a matching girdle, stockings and silk panties that clung to her firm thighs. She causally hung the jacket and skirt in the closet, intentionally leaving the closet door open. She beamed to herself as she sat on the corner of the bed; unhooked her nylons and slowly rolled them off each leg. Timons sipped his whiskey and watched her undress. She turned, winked in his direction and proceeded to remove her bra and silk panties. Folding each item and carefully laying the fineries on the chair.

Lauren turned slowly, admiring her naked form in the mirror hanging on the back of the closet door. Then Lesley handed her the whiskey. She took a sip as she continued looking into the mirror, her tall and slender body resembling an Olympic swimmer's, but with much fuller breasts and a high and tight ass. She slipped into the small twin bed and picked up Timons' new favorite book turned down on the pillow, *The New Negro: An Interpretation*. Lauren noticed a page had been dog-eared. It contained a poem by Claude McKay. She carefully closed the book, placed it on the nightstand and slowly reclined onto the bed. The sheets were cool, but she was already sweating from the summer heat.

Lesley opened the windows further and then continued undressing. The shimmering light of the full moon shined on his well-developed chest. Lauren noticed little beads of sweat glistening on his tensile hard shoulders and arms.

Lesley finished his drink in one swallow and looked down at Lauren lying on the small bed. In the moonlight he could see the sheen of her eyes and the slow curve of her waist. He flopped down on the foot of the bed and looked up at her.

"Are you hungry tonight?"

Lauren replied, "More than you know, but the question is, are you hungry?"

Lesley scooted up the bed and gave Lauren a deep, hard kiss. They wrapped their legs around each other in eagerness. Sweat dripped off their bodies in little droplets as they both became slippery to each other's touch. Lauren's heart raced as they made love.

After, as they both laid their smoking, Lauren glanced over and noticed the closet door still slightly ajar. She could clearly see the brass covered air vent on the back wall. She knew the vent was connected to the empty hotel room next door. Which allowed anyone, if the closet door was left open, an opportunity to view the entirety of Timons' hotel room. As her eyes concentrated on the fixture she suddenly noticed the two bright blue eyes of her cuckolded husband appear behind the slates of the scrolled brass, concentrating on the naked forms on the bed.

Lauren smiled with the knowledge that her true lover had watched the whole scene and would be excited for her arrival home. She grinned again as she looked back at the closet and stuffed out her cigarette.

Chapter Three

The sun was high and bright, effectively turning the streets griddle hot. The brutal heat shimmered up from the pavement and penetrated my fine wool hounds-tooth suit, roasting me slowly as I strolled out of the district courthouse towards my car parked on Hudson. The summer weather had been reasonably mild until yesterday. The temperature had been hovering in the low 90s, nice for Oklahoma in August. But now the rising mercury within thermometer on the wall of the courthouse steps indicated Mother Nature had plans to return us to our usual summer inferno.

So, I, Lou Nayland, an ex-minor league baseball player and now an underpaid private detective, strolled down the pavement feeling a bit cheap from my stint in the witness box earlier and thinking to myself *I know I'm in a rotten game and usually I can't even defend it, but it keeps me in the bucks and I don't have to slave over a desk. It's not a pretty game and nobody ever wrote a poem about it, but it's the only gig I'm suited for.*

Heading on to the car, I noticed my cotton white dress shirt I'd put on fresh this morning had already begun to become sweaty and damp as it clung firmly to my shoulders. A muggy draft of wind made it hard to breathe. I tilted my fedora farther back on my head in a vain attempt to protect the nape of my neck from the growing summer swelter. It didn't help. I noticed a hound dog curled up under a city park bench seeking shelter from the blazing heat. The sultriness of which had pushed the usual lunchtime crowd quickly back into the coolness of the buildings. The old hound and I appeared to be the only living souls remaining on the street. It was just one more hot, dirty day in what had been a very long and unprofitable week.

I'd spent the last two days in the halls of the courthouse waiting to testify in a divorce case, the result of which had been a complete waste of my time. Originally I had been retained by an over-bred filly to establish her old man was stepping out on her, a standard "wandering husband" job. What I'd learned after working on the case for a few days amounted to me discovering that her chubby car salesman husband wasn't cheating, but rather reconnecting with his illegitimate daughter he'd fathered some twenty-odd years early with a hash slinger from cow-town. Apparently the waitress had skipped town, moved out to California, and delivered a baby girl she named Veronica. This all occurring long before the fat salesman had married my client.

The direct and cross-examinations had run on for the whole opening day of testimony. Fortunately, defense counsel for the husband called me to the stand on the second day of the hearing, but as a witness for my client's spouse via a subpoena from the defendant's attorney, rather than from my client, the result meant two days of unpaid time. It wouldn't have been very jake of me to charge her for my time when my testimony tanked her case. Two hours later, the judge released me. I didn't stick around for the outcome.

Since it was still early, I'd decided I needed a baseball game to take my mind off the morning's grubby little affair. The Indians were playing the Galveston Buccaneers at 3:00 pm. So if I hurried, I still had time to buy a hot dog and make the first pitch of the game. I pulled the leather key pouch from my pocket, slid into my green Ford coupe, turned the big V-6 over, letting it idle for a minute and then pointed her nose west.

I watched the needle on the speedometer flicker up to 35 mph as I headed toward Holland Field. The stadium, located west of downtown, housed the well-manicured home field of the minor league Oklahoma City Indians.

After the game I sat in the bleachers smoking the last cigarette in my pack, reflecting on how the baseball game encapsulated a perfect afternoon for me and a majority of the other Indians fans. A breeze out of the southwest had blown on our backs throughout the nine innings and pushed out the stifling summer air from the stadium without affecting the play of the game.

The Indians' victory only reinforced my spiritual belief in the power of baseball. The game ended on a high note when the Indians repulsed the Bucs at the bottom of the ninth inning when the Indians left fielder, Johnny "The Toad," grabbed a Beaumont man's fly ball at the fence. Watching "The Toad's" leaping, winning catch and the three mustard-covered hot dogs I'd eaten had made the world right again.

For as long as I could remember, baseball had served as my only true religion, and attending the games represented my sacred attendances to high Mass. I don't recall which player or manager said it, but I liked the quote: "Baseball is like Church. Many attend, few understand."

I'd always known deep in my heart that I understood the sermon. When I was a boy, my father "Coach" Nayland took me to the ballpark every Saturday afternoon during the hot summer months. The games were mostly sandlot games played by semi-pro teams unaffiliated with major leagues. On random weekends we were privileged to see teams from the traveling Negro League. The organizations used predominantly African American and, to a lesser extent, Latin American ball players to comprise the majority of their team rosters. On one occasion we had the good fortune to see Andrew "Rube" Foster pitch a game for the Chicago American Giants. I touched the key pouch in my pocket as I reflected.

The key chain held only two things: the ignition key to the Ford and a small one inch piece of brass with inscriptions engraved on both sides of it. The front read 1916-1917, Football 7-1, Basketball 18-1, while the reverse read, S.H.S. Coach Rupert Nayland. Those close to him called him 'Rube' on the account he resembled one of the greatest left-handed pitchers of all time, Rube Waddell. The players of those winning teams had paid to engrave that piece of metal and presented it to their coach, my father, in appreciation for all he did for them both as their coach and mentor. Sadly, the old coach died three years later. This and a 14k gold plated Hamilton wristwatch were the only things my old man left me when he passed, that and his unconditional love as well as the love we shared for the game of baseball. I smiled to myself knowing dad would have loved today's game and especially the mustard-covered hot dogs.

Those afternoons with my dad watching ball games served as our version

13

of Holy Observance for the week, and the hot dogs, our holy consecrated food. Being somewhat pious regarding my views on the industry of our national pastime, I believed only I saw the sacredness of this game called baseball. I still feel. Probably because those thoughts and feelings have more to do with the Saturday afternoons spent with my dad, than my brief stint with a minor league club.

After returning to the States following the Great War, I arrived in Fort Worth early in the spring of 1919, with no job prospects, so I tried out for the local minor league ball club. To my astonishment, I made the team and obtained a fleeting stint as the first baseman with the Fort Worth Cats.

Spring games for most minor leagues were events of spiritual reverence. But as special as those early spring games were. May, June, and July were even greater for me that year. I batted .283 and knocked thirteen dingers during home stands at Panther Park. However, that all quickly changed for me when in late August I snag a line drive and attempted a throw out to third in a double play attempt on a kid from the Oilers club who was late getting off the bag. As I released the ball, however, my right arm went numb and all I could see were white fuzzy spots in front of my eyes and a burning sensation running down my arm. Back in the locker room, the team's doctor explained to me that I had torn several tendons in my shoulder. But what he really said was I'd retain full use of my arm, but I'd never play pro-ball again.

When my career ended that fall my ambitions as a ball player still felt fulfilled and even though I could no longer give a sermon from the mound, I still went to my father's and my diamond-shaped church and still felt moved by the service.

There are advantages to not being a star athlete. When you retire no one feels cheated, and gently you adjust into the real world, emotionally, as well as financially. Great athletes need a decompression chamber when the time comes to take off the uniform. They suffer withdrawal pains after the cheering stops. The fringe player doesn't miss the cheers as much, and their standard of living doesn't undergo a drastic change. The truth being even in the minor leagues, when you're playing, the wine flows and the dollies come waltzing across the green grass with big offers and pleasant smiles.

14

I stood up from my seat behind the Indians' dugout, walked out past the hot dog stand and out the turnstiles of Holland Field towards my car across the small round, brown, river pebbles of the parking lot where I had parked under a scrubby native Chickasaw plum tree.

Sliding in behind the wheel I felt my world had realigned on keel again because the game had successfully pushed away the dirty little images of the sad middle-aged car salesman and his petty, miserly wife from the recesses of my mind.

Chapter Four

The traffic on Reno thinned as I rolled up to the stop sign, turned left, pushed down on the accelerator and directed the sleek little Ford east leisurely piloting her towards downtown. I passed the county jail on West Main, as the sticky evening air blew through the car's chromed vents in a vain attempt to cool me off. Being well past closing time for the sleepy cow-town, the store fronts were darkened, but being August the streetlights appeared dark and cold. Due to the fact that my office sat closer to the ballpark than my apartment I decided to go there first, pick up the mail and close a car salesman file before heading to my place to crash for the evening.

I parked in a vacant space on Main Street on south side of my building. The space had one of those new Park-O-Meters installed on the curb. The entirety of the downtown now appeared to be totally covered up by these progressive taxing devices the city council had recently. These evil little slots, I had been told, generated thousands of dollars for the city coffers with minimal effect on an already runaway city budget at a cost of a nickel an hour to the good citizens of the city. I dropped my buffalo into the slot provided by the Park-O-Meter people and crossed the street.

My home-away-from-home was located on the northeast corner of the fifth floor in the Hightower Building at 105 North Hudson Street. The windows in my office looked out onto Hudson and the newly constructed county courthouse on the corner of First Street.

The contiguity to the marbled city center, with window exposures facing two views, symbolized an occupational necessity of proximity to possible clients due to the fact that divorce investigation paid the majority of my bills. I learned shortly after opening my business that the PI residing closest to the courthouse had the best chance of snagging newly developing divorce work as angry men and woman exited the revolving doors.

The Hightower is a quiet building of the better sort, and due to the late hour, I knew building maintenance staff had already locked the rear doors of the building at 7:00 pm. So I walked around to the front of the building to the brass front doors. I unconsciously looked up to the buildings utmost pinnacle and reflected on the things I had heard about the office complex since moving in the spring of '30.

The stock market crash in October of '29 had caused all the rich folks of the metro to lose their goods and chattels. Those losses made it tougher for the building's owners to sign on paying tenants to fill the many vacancies in their newly completed high rise. However, that situation had created a fortuitous opportunity for me five years back when I obtained a lease that locked in 1930 rates for a ten-year term, making it the cheapest little hovel in the downtown circle. It represented a genuine double-play for me, rent I could afford and an office located in the sweetest location in the metro.

I stepped through the front doors onto the white Italian marble tiles that covered the lobby floor beneath a gothic vaulted ceiling that made the lobby appear larger than it actually was. Darkly tiled square columns ran the length of the hallway to where it butted up to the four brass elevators doors near the rear of the lobby.

I pushed the black arrow on the up button and watched the brass doors slide almost silently into the walls. One of the building's several elevator operators, Linda Kealley, appeared from the recesses of the wooden lined pigeonhole of the elevator, decked out in her yellow silver button-down uniform and matching hat. She smiled up at me as she stood with her eloquent slender right hand on the button panel and her left upon the control lever, ready for action.

"Going up, Mr. Nayland?" she said with a slight lisp.

I nodded and smiled an amused grin. The attractive dishwater blonde enjoyed soft luxurious hair shingling into short curls that kept running into one another. Her face had a drawn look, making her more beautiful because she appeared more delicate. Her baby blues twinkled sardonically, even with that wisp of a smile that never left her lips. All these features labeled her a gentle person, and I never quite got over her goodness.

I stepped onto the red tiled floor of the elevator and leaned against the wooden paneled walls. Linda pushed the ceramic white button marked 5 with her usual flirtatious charm.

"How's your day going, Linda?" I asked.

"Okay, but it will be better when I get off."

When the elevator bell dinged and the doors slid apart, I smiled and thanked Linda as I handed her a Buffalo nickel. Stepping out onto the black tile flooring of the 5th floor, I glanced back over my shoulder and happily caught a wink coming from Linda as she lipped, "Thank you."

Pleased with myself, I turned down the expansive hall that ran parallel to the street below. My office was the last door on the right. The pebbled glass door panel to my office displayed letters in flecked black paint reading LOUIS "LOU" NAYLAND, PRIVATE INVESTIGATIONS. It's a reasonably sturdy door at the end of a rather shabby corridor which had not been repainted since the building had been built. I had forgotten to turn the lamps off earlier, causing a strip of golden light to shine from under the door. Taking out a skeleton key, I unlocked and pushed the door open. When it swung open, the buzzer attached began to ring and continued to do so until I closed the door behind me.

The office was a two-room suite and was in no way lovely. The golden glow now shone brightly around the inner room that had been designed as a reception area. The room contained no windows and was left open for visitors to come in, sit down and wait. The practice of which seemed to have failed due in large part to the fact that prospective clients never seemed inclined to want to wait for my return.

The office furnishings were few and old with the shabby age of second-handedness. Two burgundy covered chairs with chrome armrests sat pushed against the wall. Scattered across the cut glass coffee table were outdated copies of *Life* magazine along with the current issue of *Sporting News*. Next

18

to the chairs stood individual chromium smoking stands placed within arm's reach. Behind each stood Art Deco floor lamps that a female client had given me in lieu of payment recently. A small wooden desk and chair sat against the other wall.

Currently, they only represented my goal of affording a receptionist. Given this year's receipts and the honest fact that there's not much money in private investigations, the likely hood of additional staff seemed doubtful. A ceiling fan turned slowly overhead. A door opposite the front, on the other side of the cheap rug, the landlord had recently stenciled the word "PRIVATE" onto the door's smoked glass. I walked over and entered my workday sanctuary.

I pulled the chain to the ceiling fan, walked around the desk and dropped my weary ass into the large swivel chair. Whereby, I put my fedora down on the desk and looked around the room.

Three tall windows brightened my corner office. One faced north while two others framed my desk on the east wall. Hudson Avenue ran below these at the front of the building. The sounds of the motor traffic on Hudson rose in a muted, not unpleasant medley up to my office as I sat looking through the windows. The lights of the surrounding buildings created a will-of-wisp effect in the hazy evening sky.

My large walnut desk faced the partition door. Behind which sat my prized, longhorn hide swivel chair below the east windows. The chair represented the last thing I purchased from Texas with my final pro-ball checks. A black rotary phone sat on the right side of the desk; the blotter dead center, a steel shaded desk lamp sat in the front of the blotter. In the center of the blotter laid a blank paper tablet, slightly askew. A tin ashtray set to the left and held as many cigarette stumps as a tray of its size could expect to hold. The Westinghouse AM radio sat on a small table next to a leather couch under the north window. On one of the buff colored walls hung my framed certificate licensing Louis Nayland to pursue the calling of a private detective in the State of Oklahoma in accordance with certain-black letter regulations. A map of the city hung dangled on the south wall over a green four drawer filing cabinet.

This year's Sinclair Station calendar hung next to the map over the brass

GE fan sitting on top filing cabinet. The current month showed a voluptuous model dressed skimpily in a red wrap-around scarf. In the image, she bent slightly and playfully slipped on a sandal. The strawberry-blonde girl's eyes shone back at me along with her ruby red lips, slightly parted in a suggestive smile. No one would mistake this as a woman's office.

Failing to open the bottom left desk drawer with the tips of my fingers, I used the letter opener to gain ground. When it popped, I pulled out a superb half bottle of Scottish Oban. It was good scotch. Posh snobs describe it as having a Highland flavor. A kind of a dry, smoky style favored in the western Scottish Islands, combined with light, sweeter malts brewed in the Highlands. To me, it's just wet.

I'd acquired a taste for this particular brand during my service in the Great War. After graduating from El Dorado Junior College where I had joyfully done a two seasons stint playing baseball for Pappa Douglas, Uncle Sam came calling. But by the time I finished basic, the war had ended, I was still shipped overseas to Paris to serve out my enlistment period. While there, a Corporal Alfred Anderson, a Scotsman in the Black Watch of the Royal Highlanders and my clerk, presented me with my first bottle of Oban.

The lively red-headed kid claimed the whiskey came only from his hometown of Oban, Scotland. The little Scot explained his family sent him regular supplies of the caramel colored liquid through the Red Cross. I later learned that the distillery and the kid's hometown both sat on the west coast of Scotland. His family had stock-piled cases of the brew in 1916, when production across Britain was forbidden. His father still smuggled a couple bottles of the smooth brown whiskey through the censors by shipping the bottles with clear white labels marked "purified water."

I remember the lively little Scot laughing with great joy when he explained their scheme and suggested he believed the French Red Cross nurses, being puritanical, were racist against Scots. They truly believed that brown was the natural color of Scottish water, so they let it pass through to his unit. He sold me a fine bottle of that Scottish water for the equivalent of five shillings every week until he was shipped home to Inverness. I enjoyed every sip of every bottle, so much so in fact I now kept a bottle in my bottom desk drawer for medicinal purposes.

I snapped up one of the tumblers from the drawer and turned it lip up next to the bottle with the fine cream colored label and poured myself two fingers worth. Lacking any ice in the office, I sat back, swiveled around in my chair, and sipped it slowly and smiled to myself, though Oklahoma was still dry, one could, if they had friends, say in Scotland, acquire the appropriate elixir for a nightcap. Before I could enjoy even the first taste, my phone rang. I picked up the horn.

"Yeah," I said with the receiver pressed hard to my ear.

A musical feminine voice at the other end asked, "Is this Lou Nayland?"

Tiredly, I replied, "It's quite late, what can I do for you?"

I remained silent as I listened to the lyrical voice break slightly and become low and jerky as she explained, "Mr. Nayland, I must see you about a very confidential matter. I believe I may be in desperate trouble and I need your immediate help."

The first thought that came into my head was it was too late in the day for this kind of dame and this type of call. I took a sip of the scotch and reconsidered. "Sure," I said, "come on over. Do you have my address?"

Her voice regained its musical tenure as she sang back, "Yes, I wrote it down earlier with your phone number. I'll come to your office immediately." She hung up and a low buzz came through the earpiece.

I took another drink of the fine scotch as the phone rang again. The call reminded me of a personal matter I had forgotten to take care of. I said I would try to drop in by the end of the week, said goodbye and replaced the receiver on the cradle while I finished the drink. It was perfect scotch. I poured a second glass, toasted my redheaded military pal, and waited for the twist with the dreamy voice to appear.

Chapter Five

It was nearly 7:30 p.m. when the buzzer on the front door sounded and the distinct sound of heels clicked across the tiled floor in the reception area as the buzzer ceased. The light click-click of her Louis heels continued, then stopped close to the inner door. The smoked glass in the door prevented me from making out the exact form of my possible new client. The knob twisted, and the door swung inward, revealing a woman of class and social stature. She stood there in the door for an extended moment, smoking a cigarette as she looked around the room before staring directly at me like a hard hit line drive. I winced ever so slightly as if I had been struck by the ball, but I quickly recovered, returning her intent look.

The light from the desk lamp shone upon her face. She had a good kisser, especially when she smiled and her teeth showed white. I guessed her to be near thirty. She had a solid bosom while still maintaining the lanky and lean build of youth. She was wearing a butter yellow print dress that showed off the curves and accentuated her strong youthful lines without bragging about them.

Her sharp looking eyes sat wide apart over her chiseled cheekbones; identical to those of Sioux maidens painted in western scenes gave the impression that something clever worked behind their shiny blue surface. I had a suspicion those eyes took me in completely as I admired her outline. That single look told her more about me than I wanted her to know.

She stood there in the archway posing as warm thoughts passed over my dull brain. These thoughts clicked slowly between my ears as she took another drag and exhaled smoke in a manner that made it appear she was blowing someone a kiss. She shifted her weight to her other foot, allowing me the opportunity to take all of her in as she let a quarter inch of ash fall to the floor. I concluded she was slightly younger than my first impression. But her youth presented no barrier to her possessing a mature air. With her firmly clutching her tan Deco Day bag in her hand just below the level of her waist, I noticed the gold band on her third finger.

I smiled and let the stillness of the evening stretch out. She took several short puffs and then in a slow fluid motion snubbed out her cigarette in the chrome ashtray sitting outside the door. She had purpose in her eyes and she'd come for a reason.

"You must be Mr. Nayland?" she inquired in a voice not quite Midwestern and not quite Southern, but with hints of both.

"Why, you want to hire him?"

"Maybe, if you're him?" she replied.

"I am, but any resemblance to a drunk is just consequential." I waited for her to respond or at least give me her name—she hadn't given me one on the phone. All she had said was she needed to come speak with me, urgently.

She stood there in the doorway until I spoke. "Won't you have a seat?"

She politely stated, "Thank you," and slid warily through the doorway like a cat entering a strange room. She covered the distance across my office to an old-fashioned high back black leather chair and sat down, tilting her head slightly, and crossing her legs as she pulled her dress down over her knees and faced the windows over my shoulder. She leaned forward slightly to pull her shoe off her heel, being either an intentional or unintentional act on her part, I can't say but it had its intended effect.

Neither of us spoke as she sat somewhat nervously pulling the hem of dress up an inch or two, taking some pains to get just the right effect. Not satisfied, she removed her golden cloche hat and placed it upon my desk and leaned back so her platinum blonde hair showed to her advantage against the shiny black leather of the big chair. "Mr. Nayland, my apologies, I am a bit nervous, I have never spoken to a private detective before." She hesitated. "And I'm not quite sure where to begin."

I sat quietly, not buying her nervous speech and unwillingness to speak freely, but you never know, a lot of dames come into my office offering up the scared kitten act believing it would get them better service or a sympathetic ear. I usually humored them. I gave her my standard, rehearsed line.

"Well, miss, everyone hates used car salesmen and private detectives." She didn't respond, so I went on. "The salesman causes us anxiety on the way to acquiring something we want. Private dicks do the same. Let's see if we can work through your particular anxiety and, hopefully, I can grant you something you want."

She hesitantly nodded.

"So if you like, just start from the beginning."

Her bobbed blonde hair reminded me of Jean Harlow in the movie *The Public Enemy*. The look actually worked better on her than Harlow. She remained silent, so I pushed again. "Can I ask what's the problem that's brought you here, Mrs....?" I let the question hang.

She sensed what I was waiting for. "Pardon me. My name is Mrs. Camp, Lauren Camp. Not sure where my manners are today. Please forgive me. I'm somewhat upset. The etiquette instructors at Wellesley wouldn't approve of such lapses."

I nodded. "Camp, any chance you're related to the Indians' right fielder?"

"Yes. He is my husband, as a matter of fact. We were married last summer," she said solemnly.

She sat there motionless as I quietly thought to myself. *Normally, women who have been married for such a short period of time announced their marital status with a little more enthusiasm.*

I smoothly broke the silence. "I like your husband. He's a great ballplayer, and he seems straight all the way around." I leaned back into the large cowhide chair and proceeded. "You'll feel better if you talk it out." It was the kind of bushwa line that seemed appropriate under the circumstances.

Lauren remained restrained as the only sound came from the janitor sweeping in the hall as we both sat patiently waiting for the other to speak. I could almost read her thought process. She worried about how much to reveal to this private investigator. Was he to be trusted? Would he be able to prevent publicity regarding her delicate matter? A situation that could potentially destroy her family's reputation and everything else she held dear? And would he do so if he learned her actions were illegal?

"Can I trust you?" she asked.

"Other people have, but I don't carry references. Maybe we could start with what brought you here today and what I can do to help you."

She remained apparently tongue-tied as she sat now searching inside her purse. I too remained silent until she suddenly pulled out a silver cigarette case and withdrew a Lucky. "Let me," I said, and in a gentlemanly gesture removed an All American safety match from the box, struck it, stretched out and lit her cigarette before sitting back.

She maintained her quietude, so I attempted to swing again by speaking directly to her. "If you really need my help, you'll have to tell me what's causing such displeasure in your life."

She gave no response, so I continued more forcefully. "Okay, let's start with how you ended up on my doorstep?"

She remained speechless as a thought arouse slowly within my dull gray matter: this dame appeared a bit too contrite for one so clearly well educated, wearing expensive designer clothes and endowed with the kind of mind I suspected she possessed. Surely she wasn't afraid of nothing and nobody.

Lauren fidgeted before speaking softly. "You see, I have small domestic problem and I was told you're a man of discretion."

"Possible, but who told you I was discreet?"

"Just a man…no that's not fair, he's a man employed by my father as a security guard and his name is…" She stopped quickly before continuing, "Never mind that. Let's just say he previously worked in the sheriff's office and mentioned you might be helpful and were known to be discreet."

"Well tell him I think he's cute too," I said ruefully.

Not even a smirk crossed her lips before she continued on. "The security man stated that you could be relied on to be both honest and professional in handling delicate matters for a lady. He also indicated you have a reputation for not being bought, or at least no one to his knowledge had offered you an amount or a favor of such significant value that you considered worth selling out a client for."

I looked out the window and watched two mottle feathered pigeons court each other on the sill as I gave her a roguish response. "That's unusual for anyone in the sheriff's department to be that complementary to my line of work, except maybe the under-sheriff."

She gave no response, so I inquired further. "Brice Jackson hasn't taken to working for your family by chance, has he?"

"No," she replied.

The idea seemed to unnerve her. She took a long drag off the cigarette and rolled her other hand tighter around her clutch bag. "Our security man only gave me your name. But neither he, nor his previous employers, know anything regarding my current situation."

"Are you certain of that or just hoping?"

"You needn't be rude, Mr. Nayland," she said through her teeth.

Moving my shoulders in something like a shrug, I restated my original question. "Now, if you please recount to me your tale of woe." I let a smile appear on the last word.

She drew long upon her cigarette, crossed her legs again and she seemed to relax slightly, but her action had revealed her dress was split high up her thigh. "Mr. Nayland, I've turned it over in my head for the last two nights, trying to make up my mind, but it seems I may have no choice. No one else knows of this, yet, and it's onerous to speak it out loud to anyone else."

Lauren swallowed hard and for a second I thought she was going to button up again, but she finally came through. "You see, this has a good deal to do with my marriage and yet, in some ways, it doesn't threaten it at all." Her voice trailed off.

I cocked my right eyebrow, letting her know I was waiting for her story. I gave her my smiling eyes. It was my trick to get clients to open up, well, women clients. "Do you have something you want me to do for you or have you changed your mind?" I looked her over carefully, trying to decide whether this dame was just spooky or if she was in real danger. Either way, getting her to tell me the truth was starting to appear as difficult as convincing the school's prettiest girl to go to the spring formal.

Her golden voice was imperious, though her beautiful body remained almost inert, only the faintest movement of her breasts betrayed emotion. "Maybe you should have another drink, Mr. Nayland. You appear to be a man who can only have a real conversation with a drink in your hand."

Seeing I was still smiling she concluded dryly, "You're having fun at my expense aren't you, Mr. Nayland."

"Maybe a little," I answered.

Lauren shifted in her chair, composed herself, and then stated her thoughts with purpose. "I'm concerned if I tell you my story and you decide it's not worth your time, I won't be able to trust you to forget it?"

"I usually forget all the details to a case once it's done," I replied before she went on. "And in the alternative, if you do decide to take the case, will your ethics, since you've already mentioned you know who my husband is, therefore I'm hoping, as your client, you'll naturally protect my interests and secrecy. In short, can I trust you?"

"I believe you already know you can," I stated, but feeling she was just stalling. I had seen many a dame do the same here in my office and I had learned it was best to just waited the client out until they became scared enough to be honest. But I was tired, and her last statement had touched my last raw nerve. "We've never met, so what makes you think I would behave unethically?" I stated for shock effect. "Maybe you should go home and think on this some more." I huffed. "Because it occurs to me now, you're just wasting my time. We both should just forget we spoke and part ways."

"Now don't be nasty," Lauren said as she let the line trail off. She bit her lip, her white teeth gleaming in the evening light.

The twist was becoming charmingly confident as women often do when preparing a tactical position. Then some thought jolted her back. She bit down on the lip harder. I didn't flinch or respond, but rather let her decide if she was going to the truck or going to turn the dogs down to hunt. I raised both eyebrows and lowered my head to encourage her to continue.

She finally decided I was trustworthy, and it prompted a response whereby the woman acted with sudden decisiveness. Reopening her bag with her manicured fingers, she pulled out a folded piece of paper and spoke quickly. "I suppose I must let you at least see what has me unnerved. I can't return to my apartment and just wait for my world to crash down upon me."

Lauren handed me the letter. I observed it was on standard off-white stationary that you could find on any writing desk in any home. The letter was typed and without signature. It had been folded to fit into a half sized envelope. I read the note.

Dear Mrs. Camp:
Marriage should be honored by all, and the marriage
bed kept pure, for God will judge the adulterer and
all sexually immoral.

It is God's will that you should be sanctified: that you
should avoid sexual immorality; that...you should learn
to control your own body in a way that is holy and honorable,
not in passionate lust like the pagans, who do not know God.

Do not let your unfaithfulness bear the fruit of horns upon
your husband's head. Your adulterous lips do drip honey,
but I know you to speak bitterly and to be unholy.

Does your husband know the evil you countenance?
Repent or the Lord shall have you stoned in the streets.

Trying not to respond with my usual dry wit, I stated, "He's sure got a religious bent to his writings, doesn't he?"

Lauren didn't reply, so I said, "It's been a while since I've been in Sunday school, so my Bible study is a little weak. But the first verse sounds like it came from the New Testament rather than the Old, possibly the book of Hebrews? There's some guessing on my part there. The second verse I can't place exactly, but it still sounds biblical. The third verse is different from the first two. It sounds like it comes from a play or literature." I knew it was a line from *Othello*, but I wasn't ready to reveal my hold card that I had actually read more than one book. It was best she attempted to explain.

28

The well-heeled socialite snubbed out her second smoke and found her voice. "Very good, Mr. Nayland. You may not be the Neanderthal one expects to find in your line of work." She continued on, "I wasn't sure of the source either. But you're correct, it's biblical, although I doubt these particular verses ever come up during a Sunday school class. I had to look them up myself."

Lauren proceeded. "The first two verses both come from the New Testament in the Books of Hebrews and Thessalonians. You're right about the third line; it does come from a play, Shakespeare's *Othello*, actually." She cast a knowing smile over the desk at me.

"Your pen pal seems to be a more fervent believer than most people you find in the aisle of St. Luke's," I exclaimed. She nodded in the affirmative.

She didn't speak further, so I asked, "Did you receive this by messenger or via the mail service?"

"By the post," she said softly.

"Was it inside an addressed envelope?" I asked as the murmur of traffic pasted under the window.

She nodded again, swallowing in such a way her throat constricted with the action. "Would you like to see it?"

"Please," I replied.

Lauren reached into her purse and handed me a smooth white envelope which had been opened with a very sharp knife. The typed address on the front read: *Lauren Camp, Mayfair Apartments, Oklahoma City, Oklahoma.* The postmark was faded and slightly askew but legible: *Oklahoma City, OK, August 1.*

I turned the envelope over in my hand and asked, "I take it your husband hasn't seen this?"

"No, he hasn't. He was traveling with the team at the time of its arrival."

I was starting to think she was the kind of dame that gave marriage a bad name and thought about asking if any of this was accurate. I figured it was or she wouldn't be dishing this story with such concern, but I didn't want her to walk out just yet. My interest was piqued.

Mrs. Camp stood up, lit another smoke, and walked to the window. The evening sun reflected off the courthouse windows, the soft light casted enough brightness to allow me to admire her silhouette through the thin yellow cotton dress. Something about her gave a hint of feline efficiency in the way she had placed herself against the large window to achieve the best effect from the outside light, she took a long drag and exhaled as she asked, "Any thoughts on what you just read?"

I attempted to read her thoughts before speaking. "I don't mean to be indelicate, and I apologize if I am, but is there any truth or proof to these allegations?"

There was a long pause while she met my eyes. "There might be something in it." She sighed with a nervous exhale. "Or, someone seems to believe they know my secrets."

I spun in my office chair and stared up at her as she inhaled the blue smoke up her nostrils and then blew perfect smoke rings into the slow turning ceiling fan. I observed that she was well formed and possessed long shapely legs that most men waited a lifetime to have wrapped around them.

"That's a curious allegation," I said before asking, "so what are you exactly trying to hire me to do?"

"Isn't that obvious?"

"Not at all, but I assume you want to discover who sent the letter, and what? Turn it over to the district attorney's office for prosecution? If not that, it's not clear what I can do for you, so maybe its best you spell it out."

"Fine, and no, obviously I don't want to involve the authorities or I would have gone to the district attorney's office," she said through the smoke escaping between her teeth. "What I need is for you to make it stop, God damn it."

Her curse was a complete break in character and composure. She started to speak and then halted mid-word and glanced downward toward her shoes and continued to do so for several moments like she was fascinated by them.

The beautiful client looked back through me with her baby blues that had just flared gun-barrel-gray as the word "NO" rushed over her lips. Her deadly look was unexpected in a woman of her obvious breeding. I've dealt with handfuls of nervous wives, who worried some dirty little secret would harm their standing or their marriage, but this dame was playing it too close to the vest for my liking. Suddenly she cooled as quickly as she had flared.

I smiled at her. "Go on." I picked up the letter opener and traced a pattern on the desk blotter as I listened to her story.

"Neither I, nor my family can afford to have this scandal exposed." Her voice changed, becoming warm and almost coaxing. "To be honest, Mr. Nayland, the scandal and headlines could cause a minor difficulty for me, but it wouldn't be ruinous to my marriage. But I won't explain that fact to you. However, there are elements of my infidelities that could be far more damaging to my family's reputation and standing in the community than any damage to my marriage."

This was a new twist on a tale as old as the bible. She clearly wasn't concerned about her husband discovering her unfaithfulness, only her family finding out. The little gears in my head told me there was something more to her story. I pursued a different line of questioning.

"Your husband…" I hesitated briefly. "Is he the jealous type?"

Her steady blue eyes regarded me with a slight twinkle. "Not at all, he's a very soft spoken man. He's a good man. We keep no secrets from one another. I can say that with certainty. We know all of each other's secrets and have come to terms with such."

Hm. She was quite persuasive. I pressed further. "Are you in love with him? Your husband, I mean?"

Lauren considered the question for several seconds before the cadence of her speech almost faltered as she attempted to speak. "I love him to the depth and breadth of my very soul." Her words ghosted off just above a whisper as she turned and faced me, I saw the hot spark form in her eyes as her very spirit filled the room like Hera atop of Mt. Olympus declaring her jealously of Zeus. "I love Johnny, the way you love just one time! Can you understand that, Mr. Nayland?"

"Okay, I believe you." I felt she needed to hear me say those words.

I directed the conversation back to the letter. "The letter suggests there is a third party. If it's true, is your reluctance to give me a full account about the parties concerned because you're protecting a lover or your husband?

31

Or both?" I hoped I hadn't over-reached.

She stood there smoking and watching the sunset out my window, evidently considering her answer. Our conversation hadn't relieved her anxiety, and she appeared to still be in a state of torment. She was, like most women I knew, a keeper of secrets.

I pushed harder. "Do you love your paramour?"

I sensed a shudder rippling over her as she gave me a flashing, haughty look. "I'm restless at times and require distractions from life's day-to-day doldrums, but love, definitely NOT!"

I knew exclamations blurted out at the moment of shock have only a forty percent validity rating, but I remained silent and let her continue.

"You might describe it as a form of addiction, but it doesn't really matter, does it, because I'm hoping you're going to handle it? Either way, Mr. Nayland, I can live with the disgrace to me and even to my family, but I would never forgive myself for what it would do to my husband professionally. I'm begging you, please, find whoever is behind this mess and make it or them go away."

Now it's "Lou," I thought "Well, Mrs. Camp, please have a seat. I'll need some guidance as to where to start."

She half-turned and sat limply in the chair while putting out what remained of her snipe into the ashtray. "What can I tell you that may help?"

"What's your paramour's name?"

She remained calm, but her attitude indicated a cold determination to keep from me that personal detail as she spoke. "No, I'm not ready to give you that information yet, Mr. Nayland."

There was such finality in her voice that I dared not press the matter further. "Okay, let's try another avenue then. Do you know anyone who may have actual evidence that could support the claims in the letter? More importantly, are there people who could possibly testify to such things?"

She considered the matter for several seconds before asking, "To actual proof? No, I really can't think of any, however, as to persons who could speak of it? Yes, there are probably half-dozen or so individuals who could give damaging statements."

"A half-dozen." I sighed. "Well, let's start with ones that are more likely than not to have damaging information."

She hesitated, took out another cigarette, which I lit. "There's no one in my family's circle that would have any idea or even know the people who might know, and my brother doesn't frequent the kind of places people in the know hang out. He's what most people describe as a prude."

"Okay, so you don't believe it's anyone in your family. Is there anyone in your family's church circle that might have associates that have friendships or business connections that cross out of your usual social circle?"

Lauren took a drag and said confidently, "I doubt very much that the fine members of St. Luke's church would associate in any way with the people that know the details of my indiscretions." She took another long puff. Started again, then hesitated as she leaned back in her chair and flashed her large pale blues like a newborn calf in my direction.

"I really am putting my life in your hands now, Mr. Nayland." She sighed deeply before continuing. "Because the people who would most likely have knowledge of my nocturnal wanderings all live in or work in the Deep Deuce."

I had spent my youth traveling with professional ballplayers, so nothing sexual much surprised me anymore. It might also be said that I had driven a few balls to the fence over the years myself, and that some of my hits had actually allowed me to touch all the bases in the game of love. I wasn't shocked by her bold statement of interracial nocturnal activities, but it certainly wasn't what I expected to hear from an uptown girl.

Either way, I kept my growing uneasiness to myself, because I now understood how the identity of her lover could cause backlash across the city, especially to the standing of her family and particularly her husband.

I looked at her without betraying my concerns and added, "I don't believe the person who sent this letter is a professional grifter. It's too personal. I suspect its someone closer to you than you realize, or it's a person who knows one or more of the parties involved. So again, I ask, can you give me a least one name to start?"

She gave me nothing.

33

"How about the name of the musician you're involved with?"

"Why makes you believe my lover's a musician?"

I gave her a half-smiling but perceptive glance. "First, it's obvious that a swell-talking musician would be just the type of man who'd be involved with a good looking woman like you. And second, you mentioned the Deep Deuce area as a possible backdrop to your little love nest."

She stared back and gave me an insightful smile. "Possible, but I don't think I'll tell you that just yet, Mr. Nayland. And besides, if you're half as good as I hear you are, you're likely to discover that on your own as well as who sent this letter and how to put an end to this sordid interlude without me divulging all my secrets. Call it a woman's privilege for now." The statement was cordial enough, but her attitude indicated a cold determination to keep from revealing the name of her lover.

I put my clasped hands on the desk and spoke firmly. "If you want to help yourself in this matter, Mrs. Camp, you're going to have to be more forthcoming. Because believe me, I'm only trying to protect you. As you have undoubtedly learned here today, I've a tendency to speak plainly and frankly with my clients, and I expect them to do the same. But like most of my beliefs, I often expect too much. I'm usually disappointed. I'm getting used to it."

She looked at me now with a little more seriousness. "All right, other than my paramour's name, what details would you like me to provide you with?"

The canary in her started singing names. "I guess the doorman at the Aldridge theater. His first name is George, I don't recall his surname. Then there's Thomas, the night clerk at the Littlepage Hotel. Possibly some bartenders or band members from the Aldridge or Ruby's Grill may have some clue. I must tell you that my time there is limited, and for the most part, very private. I hope that is enough for now, or at least enough for you to get started?"

She wasn't so much a Wellesley lady to not suddenly come out of her chair and arrange herself appealingly on top of my desk, lean in and give me a fierce and purring smile. Her maneuvers provided me with a better view of her perfectly formed breasts, so I let her speak. "You will try to help me, won't you, Mr. Nayland?"

I wasn't about to let this payday walk out the door, but it was always best to be honest about the money up front. "In a situation like this, it will take time. And although I like your look and your voice, I do this for a living. I get thirty bucks a day and, of course, expenses."

"I see, and what would be the nature of these expenses you'd incur?"

"There are always little things that come up here and there. Sometimes it's the cost of canary food to encourage little birds to sing a melody of information I require on your behalf. Sometimes it's something as mundane as cab fare at a moment's notice. Like I said, lots little things come up."

"But I would like to know," she said firmly.

I grinned with boyish charm. "You'll get it all in a nicely printed invoice done up in black and white at the conclusion of our business. At which time you can object to any items you believe are outside the scope of my employment."

"How much of a retainer do you expect for a job like this?" she inquired.

I responded professionally, "It will cost two to three hundred dollars a week, and with what you've given me to this point, it could take at least a month. So let's start with a week's worth of expenses and incidentals."

She looked at me dubiously. "My family is rich, that is true, Mr. Nayland, but I am not. Johnny and I live on what baseball pays, but it only pays during the season. I do receive an allowance from my family, but my grandmother controls it quite tightly, and to be honest, it's not much. I have some funds tucked away I can use."

I smiled politely and inquired, "Now that you bring that up, is there a way to meet your family for some indirect questions without raising suspicions?"

"Let me consider that for a moment." After a long pause, she made a suggestion. "Maybe I can square a guest pass to one of my grandmother's social lunches. I could introduce you as an old baseball buddy of Johnny's."

I nodded in approval as she continued, "I'll let you know the time and place after I have sowed some seeds."

She then spilled the contents of her purse on the desk. Lipstick, cigarettes, a well-worn address book full of phone numbers, another envelope, some hair pins, a roll of bills and some keys.

Lauren picked up the roll and peeled six fifties from the roll and pushed them toward me. "Will this do?" she asked.

I took the bills, counting them quickly, but as I did so, I couldn't help but notice what she hadn't intentionally spilled out of the bag and which was of much more interest to me. What I'd caught was a glimpse of a dark blue colt auto purse gun, but I didn't let on as I placed my right palm over the three C's of lettuce and pulled them into my top desk drawer. "Yes, thank you."

My new paying client refilled her purse as I clasped my hands together and asked, "Where can I reach you if it becomes necessary?"

She pulled one of my cards from the desk holder, flipped it over and wrote her telephone number: 7-0515 at the Mayfair Apartments on the back. I recognized the place and knew it was the main digs where all the young toffs set up playing house.

"What's your apartment number, just in case I need to slip in unnoticed for a chat if something important comes up?"

"Twenty, it's on the top floor. Take the back stairs, please."

I admitted through my teeth, "I can't guarantee I'll have results for you this week, or even three."

She straightened herself in the chair and asked, "Why is that, Mr. Nayland?"

"Because basically you still kind of have me working in a vacuum due to your request for discretion in this matter. The result of which means there're are some sources that can't be used by the very virtue they tend to leak in every direction when you tug on them. But with that said, I'll run a quiet check on your suggestions as well as make some inquires of my own with private confidential informants and get back to you by the end of the week."

She gathered herself up, said thank you without moving her lips, and whirled gracefully towards the door. "Just remember one thing," she said. "I'm your client. You violate my confidence, I'll sue you for damages and see that you lose your license."

Not the most cordial parting remark. Still, by and large, I think I preferred it to "Have a nice day."

When she had gone, I leaned back and watched the fan overhead slowly turn. I casually reached down to the lower left drawer, pulled out the bottle of brown plaid and filled my tumbler. I thought to myself that the well-heeled Mrs. Camp hadn't provided me with as many details as I would have liked, thus making it impossible to conclude the case to her satisfaction. However, it still held the possibility of a nice little fee with only a slight hint of trouble, considering the woman's social status. I paced my office for twenty minutes, deliberating on how I should proceed. Once decided, I finished my drink, grabbed my coat and followed the path of the blonde out the door.

Chapter Six

Anybody hanging around the Oklahoma County Sheriff's office first thing on a Monday morning is either a pimp putting up bail, a boozer let go after his weekend bender or a private dick. Since I wasn't wearing a zoot suit, sporting a brightly colored wide brim hat, or drunk, an observer would guess I was a PI grasping at straws.

When the under-sheriff calls you on the weekend and tells you to come to the office on Monday, he must have a reason and you don't ignore the "request." So, I parked my car near my office at the Hightower and hiked around the corner the two blocks west to Main and Dewey where the jail and sheriff's offices stood.

I strolled under the bricked arched entryway, walked up to the main floor, stopped, eyed the duty sergeant and proceeded straight to his raised desk situated in the middle of the poorly lit squad room.

The large rectangular room reminded me of the grimy look and odor of a public institution where nobody lived. The sergeant heard my wingtips clip along the tile floor and looked straight through me and without even acknowledging me, said, "Jackson's looking for you; get your ass up there."

I cut through the booking area and took the stairs two at a time to the second floor onto a freshly scrubbed corridor smelling of antiseptic. Walking towards the row of offices I noticed Effie Darling, the under-sheriff's girl Friday, who was gloomily fingering the day's filings of lost and stolen property. Numerous wallets had been reported taken from the midtown section of the city. Their only chance of recovery lay across the hall in the offices of the pickpocket squad. A robbery in Packing-town and the usual assortment of missing handbags, wrist-watches and briefcases served as testimonials to their owners' forgetfulness. Darling studied them all spread out over the open drawer of a green filing cabinet while at the same time running sentry over Jackson's office door.

Darling was a little woman who burned twice the calories of any large farmer's wife, due to the fact that she was always in constant motion. Even at rest, her mind went a mile a minute, like a wall clock with a spring wound too tight. Men noticed her pretty, slim and well portioned body; closing in on forty-five, with long brunette hair, and high-arched eyebrows giving her a startled look, all of which allowed her to maintain an air of sexuality, which only time and experience can bestow. She cultivated a reputation as a renowned herring of a woman who never let the secrets of the office pass her lips. I've always been a sucker for a pretty face with nice hips for a background.

She watched me approach, looked at me primly, with a finger to her lips. "He's on the phone, but he's waiting for you. Go on in, flatfoot."

I walked to the office door just off the side of her desk, tapped softly on the pebbled glass panel, waited a moment, turned the knob worn smooth by a thousand oily hands and entered. Brice Jackson sat in a large leather office chair behind an even larger mahogany desk, talking on the phone. He was speaking in his usual southwestern drawl while flipping a silver dollar in the air with his right hand and catching it before it hit the desk. He grunted and pointed to a chair in front of his desk.

On the wall behind him hung two black framed portraits, one of Sheriff Stanley Rogers, a man of influence within this state, especially since becoming the president of the Oklahoma Sheriff and Police Officers' Association. He wore his white felt fedora in the picture. I reflected that I'd never seen the man or a picture of him without it. The other was a portrait of President Franklin D. Roosevelt. These two powerful men stared back at me with conviction. Jackson's white felt cowboy hat hunkered atop the rack in the corner. Two standard government chairs sat aligned perfectly in front of the desk. I parked down opposite of him and waited for the inquisition to start. He showed no surprise. He stared at me blandly over the receiver of the phone pressed to his ear.

Jackson owned a look right off a Marine recruitment poster that had been so popular in the Great War. His perfectly cropped dirty blonde hair had a dusting of tweedy gray at the temples, which women loved. A gleaming shaved face and a severe look highlighted his chiseled features. He wore a crisp white gabardine shirt with tan slacks.

I'd first met the under-sheriff when working as a flatfoot for the Fort Worth Police Department after my minor league baseball stint. The department had sent me up to the Big Friendly to collect a prisoner wanted for forging war bonds in Texas. My involvement with him had been short, but when I moved to the city, we bumped into each other from time to time and we liked the same lunch spots. Over the years, we grew friendly enough for him to throw me a case or two when it wasn't in his department's purview.

He hung up the phone, placed the silver dollar in the top drawer, walked to the window and in his usual calm twang asked, "What you working on this week, Lou?"

Even with his drawl, he spoke well and deadly when the occasion called for it, but over time I had learned he possessed the manners of a choir boy and a preacher's morality to boot.

Instinctively I knew from his tone he wasn't fishing for news, but rather digging for worms. I spoke cautiously. "A couple of wandering husband jobs mostly."

He turned towards me and gave me his best Parris Island glare. "I heard a rumor you may be working for one of the swells from uptown."

I didn't take the bait. I stood there in silence until a growl of discomfort issued from his lips. "That's a little far afield from your usual haunts, isn't it?"

Apprehension slowly arose inside my head as I wondered how he had learned that tidbit so quickly. I rubbed a knuckle thoughtfully behind my ear as I sat mum and studied his lean, hard-bitten face. He removed a cigarette from a cellophane wrapped packet and began rolling it between his fingers, stretching out the silence that fell between us.

Hesitantly, I broke the spell. "Let's say I had. Surely this isn't the place to

40

discuss it. Besides, it looks like you have a lot on your desk this morning. Why don't I buy you a lunch steak at Cattleman's, say around one o'clock? I'll feel more like conversing with food in my stomach."

"That serious of a thing, is it?"

I had the gut feeling he knew more than he was letting on. "Not really, but if I did have a swell on the hook, I don't think they would appreciate me having an official conversation regarding their interests in a government building."

Jackson looked unimpressed. "Huh, maybe I'll have a couple of my guys follow you around a few days, Lou, and acquire the answers for myself."

I shrugged. "I suppose you could, but I know the alleys of this cow-town better than any of your mugs and you know they're not capable enough to stay on my tail to be any good or...you could just beat me to get the story," I stated with a smirk.

"I might enjoy doing just that." Jackson grinned back.

I raised an eyebrow with a finely drawn expression upon my face and proposed, "Just meet me for lunch and we'll catch up on the latest Indians games."

"Cut it," Jackson chopped in. In a quieter voice, he finished with, "Scram. I'll see you at 12:30."

I got up before he changed his mind; reached the door and left before he said another word. I steered my way out of the building and back to my office.

Chapter Seven

I left the office as the courthouse clock struck 12:00, made the drive over to Packing Town where the café sat on South Agnew just south of the North Canadian River that cut the city in half.

The Ford clipped along Agnew towards Cattlemen's until its tires shuddered onto the pitted road of the cattle yards. The thick cloying smell of the cattle pens made my eyes sting. Glancing down the street I watched as the dungaree wearing field hands, out of work, high-heeled cow-pokes, and the local bankers that financed the cattle trade all swaggered through the bright blazing noonday sun. Only the bankers moved with any purpose.

Cattleman's Café, the favorite steak house of the locals, was situated on the main drag of cow-town. The dinner had a distinct atmosphere that couldn't be found on the main streets of the Big Friendly. The place provided lunch and dinners for plant workers, hungry cowboys, bankers and ranchers in town for the cattle sales. It also happened to be Jackson's favorite place to have lunch. He enjoyed the steaks and the patrons that frequented the place more than the uptown cafes that serviced the city's swells. Since our first lunch there, it had thereafter acquired the force of custom, so that any change of venue would have been an innovation.

Packing Town was the slower moving part of town, whose smell of money carried on the wind and reminded everyone how our little town had begun. I pulled my coupe into an empty space across the street from the café entrance. Crossing the street, I swore as I tried to avoid the fresh horse and cattle droppings that lined the street. I opened the heavy glass café front door and stepped in.

Five of the twelve stools that lined the red laminated lunch counter were taken. Sheriff Jackson was already sitting in one. His white Stetson was turned upside down on the empty seat to his right. No real cowboy every laid his lid right side up; it would break the cut of the brim, and Jackson breathed real cowboy through and through.

Chrome trimmed stools lined the lunch counter, each covered in faux burgundy leather. Opposite the counter ran two rows of booths, both the seats and backings were covered in the same leather. The walls were paneled in stained wood, which stood in contrast to the chrome fittings of the tables. The owners had hung black and white photos of cattle drives and cowboys in the center of each of the panels.

Jackson saw me walk in, put his cigarette out in the tin tray and pushed it towards the glass shakers of salt and pepper. He pointed to the empty seat next to him. I removed my hat, placed it on the rack by the door and proceeded across the lime green tiled floor and took a seat.

A poorly bleached-blonde hash slinger with soft gray eyes containing small glints of color hardened on the corners by spectacles stood patiently behind the counter, looking bored. She wore a dull brown cotton dress tied at the waist with a white server's apron. She gave us a cheerful smile and asked, "Something to cool your innards, boys?"

Jackson drawled, "Two ice teas will be fine, thanks." As he spoke, I heard a remote passionate voice serenading in Spanish coming from the kitchen. I caught the words for love and death. *Amor, Morte.*

When the waitress went to retrieve our drinks, he spoke in a whispering tone out of the corner of his mouth. "Care to fill me in now on what or who you got yourself mixed up with, Lou?"

I didn't respond as I considered who in Jackson's office had given my name to Mrs. Camp and most likely tipped him off that I had been retained. I remained silent as the waitress returned with our ice teas and put them before us as she gave a casual wink in Brice's direction. "What you two handsome men going to have?"

She smiled a playful smile at each of us as she pushed her pencil in and out of her hair, searching for an undetermined itch. She stood there patiently in front of the glass display case that held homemade pies; I could detect the faint smell of apple and cinnamon wafting through the air.

Brice spoke up. "Give us each a lunch steak with taters."

Her smile disappeared as she took the order down on a greased-stained ticket pad, walked back down along the counter to where the cook stood in front of a grimy, stained grill and stuck our order into the wire ticket stand over the sizzling stove.

We sat in silence, as befits two men who know each other intimately, as our waitress continued down to the other end of the counter to pour water into the empty glasses of other patrons before I tilted my head towards his ear. "So what do you know about my recent case referral from Heritage Hills?"

"Not much, just that big city money hired you to look into some personal family business."

Brice stopped there, so I continued. "To be honest, it's not much of a case really, just a little snooping around regarding some possible domestic troubles."

Jackson nodded but remained quiet, so I went on. "Confidentially, I was approached by the daughter of one of the city's wealthy oil families concerning a letter that made vague threats regarding some activities that might be dangerous to her martial relationship."

Brice shook his head. "So just more peeper work?"

With a slightly embarrassed smile, I spoke in my defense. "You know, it's slow at the office right now and her story made me a bit curious, so I'm going to look into it."

Slight disbelief crossed over Brice's face as he shook his head. "You were right earlier, it sounds more like the usual dodgy divorce work you do and not something that should be handled officially through my office."

"That's likely, but you know me, Brice. If something changes, you'll be the first to know."

"Yeah, right." He grinned as he sipped tea. "Ah hell, better you than me, because any official investigation makes the swells mighty uncomfortable and ruffles their feathers when my guys start asking questions all over town, especially in some gossipy love triangle. Then they call the county politicians, which in turn means the heat trickles down to me. Besides, from what I've seen, the posh usually deserve the trouble they make for themselves, so better you than me." He smirked.

Brice quickly stopped smirking and asked, "Think you can help them out?"

I spoke in a lower tone. "I'm not sure yet. The young lady hasn't given me much to go on, but I'll dig around a few days to see if what she did give me has any truth in it."

I sipped my tea, deciding whether I should say anymore. The Deep Deuce element had me both intrigued and concerned. Maybe having some help from the law could speed the case up. I knew Brice had dirt on just about every family of interest in the city.

I looked back at him as he quietly waited for me to continue. "To be truthful, Brice, my client's suggestions are limited at best and I haven't any real clues for which rock to start looking under first."

Brice didn't seem eager to add anything, so I suggested, "I could use your help if you could throw me a bone, off the record, of course; and mum's the word regarding the Davis family."

Brice took a long look at me and said, "The Davis family, huh? Sure you want to get yourself involved with those people? The old man has a ruthless past, some say." I caught a dawning of doubt on his face.

I gave an understanding nod, so he continued. "The repercussions, if you go afoul, may make you unsuitable to remain in this town."

I acknowledged my understanding of the possible backlash of any investigation surrounding the family, so he proceeded. "Honestly, Lou, most of what I got you could read in old newspapers, but I'll give you some odd tidbits not found in the papers, if you think it might help."

I nodded as he set upon his story. "Seems that old man Davis acquired oil leases under tribal land in Osage County in the late teens and twenties and made him a bundle. There is some scuttlebutt that he may have had some connection to the Osage Indian murders in his acquisition of those leases, but he was never investigated or charged."

I uncrossed my arms and played with my lighter on the counter as he continued. "Anyway, his end of the deal made him one of the three richest men in town. Some say he was making $64,000 every twenty-four hours at his peak. Either way, he wanted everyone to know he prospered, so he donated a load of green to the University down in Norman for some new athletic stadium. My guess is he must have been born with two lucky horseshoes in his hands or he's truly as ruthless as some suspect."

Brice then proceeded to give me what he considered several indisputable facts. "On the personal side, he and his wife Della Mae had four children. Their youngest, a daughter, married a local pastor and moved up north. Poor folk, old man Davis didn't approve of her marrying beneath their family's station. So the daughter and her new husband moved to New York City to start a family and work. They were living in the city after the War when the Spanish Flu pandemic swept the country. The daughter and her husband both died, leaving the two kids, a boy and a girl. After the funeral, the grandkids came back here to live with old man Davis and Della Mae. I think the kids were nine or ten when it happened. Anyway, the grandparents raised the girl until she went off to university somewhere back east." I chuckled to myself at how Jackson always referred to women under forty as girls.

Brice went on, "Best I can recall he stayed local and went to the University in Norman and is a teacher or something now here in the city."

I decided to push him for more pertinent facts. "Has there been business or legal troubles in their history? You know something a family of their standing would want to keep in the closet?"

Brice hesitated. "Far as I can tell, the grandparents are good Methodists. They've been members of St. Luke's from the beginning. Other than church ice cream socials and pie dinners, they attend few social events, the ones they do are mostly political ones. The old man appears to like the idea of the power behind the throne and is into dabbling in local and state politics. He's also a huge supporter of Roosevelt and is currently pushing for a little 'New Deal' for Oklahoma."

Lunch arrived. Each plate held a large sirloin that touched the edges of the plate. Fried potatoes were served on the side. Miss Charming also brought a basket of steaming hot, buttered dinner rolls. The conversation lulled as we ate. Brice started packing the food in like an infantryman after a forty mile hike and left hanging any further discussion of the Davis family. He remained tight-lipped until he used one of the last hot dinner rolls to clean the steak juice from his plate.

He waited for me to finish as he lit a cigarette, took a long drag and then accidently knocked ash off onto the counter. He bent his head to blow it off and then slowly started to speak. "You wouldn't know this part because it was before your time here, but most the long timers of the city know that the old man was heavily involved, politically, with the group favoring impeachment of Governor John Walton back in '23."

"Yeah, I was still a flatfoot in Fort Worth then."

Brice bobbed his head, wiped his lips with a napkin and continued. "From what I heard, Walton picked a fight with the Klan when he declared martial law in Okmulgee and Tulsa counties after the Tulsa Race Riots in '21." Brice shook his head. "A damn mess and a national embarrassment. Anyway, the story goes that the legislature started up impeachment proceedings on the governor for over-reaching his authority. It was also rumored that Davis used his newly found wealth to buy the votes they needed. Whereby, Davis and his group succeeded in forcing Walton out of office in disgrace. But what's not published, and what everyone knows is there was substantial Klan involvement in the process, at least by the eastern senators."

I sat in silence and let him carry on. "The editor of *The Black Dispatch*, Roscoe Dunjee, wrote extensively on it and still publishes stories about those connected to it every now and then. But of course the city newspapers never carried that part of the story."

I sat there, soaking it all in. Slowly understanding why Lauren Camp was worried. Grandfather may have Klan ties, and she's playing around in Deep Deuce.

Brice took another draw, blew the smoke out through his nostrils and continued, "I know it's all before your time here, but it's pretty common knowledge around the city that the Old Man had a huge behind the scenes hand in the formation of Deep Deuce and segregating the minority community to the eastside of downtown back in the mid-teens. And it was widely reported that he and his cronies at the City Planning Commission sold the whole concept as a progressive plan that benefited all the communities of the city. However, the real truth though is somewhat different. In reality, the Commission just wanted the blacks pushed out of downtown so they selected an area on the Canadian River flood plain around NE 2nd for the coloreds to reside. But to prove how progressive they were, they built the coloreds a new high school on High Street and named it Douglas. But everyone of any color here-about knows it was just a scam to segregate the city." He took another draw and went quiet.

I deliberated on what he said and decided to put a pin in it. Knowing what he had just told me was common knowledge and not necessarily helpful. I needed some definitive dirt, the kind usually found only in innuendo and rumor.

The canary had mentioned the Deep Deuce and her family in a much different direction. So I decided to test the waters and inquire further what Brice knew about the Camp woman, if anything. "What do you know about the girl or her brother? Do they have any connections to the Deep Deuce?"

Brice finished his cigarette and stubbed it out in the tin tray. "As far as I know, the girl's clean, well educated, doesn't have to work due to her family's money. She married some ball player. Some guys just draw aces all the way around. At any rate, the young couple lives in one of those nice apartments in Mayfair off 13th Street. The husband is the right fielder for the Indians and appears to be as clean as the Pope on Sunday, from what I can make out."

I nodded as he went on, "Anyway, from what I hear she's a good wife who sits in the players' wives' box, at all the Indians' home games and cheers him on. At least, that's what I've seen every time I catch a ballgame."

Brice leaned back on his boot heels, "Care for a mound secret? She's the best looking dame over twenty-five in town. She could make a Catholic priest convert to the Protestant faith, just so he could acquire a wife like her."

Brice pulled out a gold Elgin pocket watch and flipped open the cover. I caught a glimpse of a stunning blonde pictured on the inside I knew to be his wife. He registered the time, swung his legs out from under the counter, and prepared to stand up.

"Lou, is that it? I've got to meet Sheriff Rogers and some police detectives at 2:30."

"Before you go, what do you know about the brother, you got anything on him?" I cautiously asked him.

Brice settled back into his chair but spoke hurriedly. "He's a college kid who teaches somewhere and as far as I know he's pretty clean. But you know brothers and sisters. They tend to react to one another like oil and water and in their case this is especially true. Apparently several years back there was a little ruckus between them. Allegedly the fracas got so out far of hand the sister actually filed assault and battery charge against him." He said with a slight mischievous grin on his lips. "Anyway the metro police hauled the brother in for smacking her around, mostly because he bruised her face up so badly. Presumably the neighbors called it in, saying it sounded like two cats were tearing each other up." He stated with bemusement before he continued, "Anyway it happened when both of them where back for summer break. The story goes that when the sister wasn't working for the family's firm, she spent a lot of time downtown listening to music and that was a sore spot for the brother. Normally, I wouldn't pay attention to matters of this nature, but some of the boys like sharing the story."

I sat looking at the pies in the case, as he went on, "Supposedly a couple weeks into the summer break, the girl started seeing a young mixed race trumpet player. Who being from Chicago was unaware such a situation was taboo around these parts," he said with an arched brow. "In any event, this Northern cat was dumb enough to come to the house to pick her up for a date to the movies or something, and all hell broke loose when the brother answered the door. The two then had a heated exchange, that nobody heard, after which the young musician wised up and left pretty quickly."

I muttered, "Interesting."

He nodded in agreement before continuing, "As this was happening the girl comes out on the porch and starts screaming at her brother and apparently they made quite a scene."

I didn't move or asked a question. I just let him weave his tale.

"When two city prowlers pulled up to the curb, the brother and sister were still screaming at each other in the front yard. You'd think those kids would have known better."

Shaking his head, Brice went on again, "The cops broke them apart and the girl had a shiner over her left eye that was already turning shades of black and blue. She was stomping madder than a wet hen. She kept screaming she wanted to press charges against her brother while the cops held her back that." He smiled as he finished up,

The waitress came back offering to fill our glasses. We both shook our heads no as Brice continued to speak. "Eventually it quiets down, and the family sweeps the whole thing under the rug. Assumingly they paid off the nosy neighbors to keep quiet and for the newspapers not to publish any accounts of the incident. And there's no official report on the call on a file anywhere." Brice concluded, "To my thinking it was more than some spoiled little girl being told she couldn't do something, more like a young woman trying to act all modern with her coastal attitude and ways. Either way, the family sent her packing back to school pretty quick."

I indicated I understood why with a slow nod and said, "Well at least you had one good story in you worth me paying for lunch."

Brice put his Stetson on and added, "But you know, she's apparently still into the jazz music scene. My boys tell me they've seen her big Packard parked down in Deep Deuce on the weekends. It appears she's down there on the nights when the Indians aren't playing or are out of town. Guess she still likes all that jazz and glitter."

I said to myself, "I knew she liked far more than the music, but didn't let on, nor did I like the conclusion my mind was drawing from the growing facts. My actual knowledge of the sister's love for jazz and those who played it, along with the brother-sister altercation, the grandfather's political battles and the growing possibility that father and son seemed to share a similar racial bias were all indicative of trouble simmering within their clan and possible reasons for one of them to blackmail Lauren."

So before Brice left, I decided I'd fish with him awhile longer and I casted cautiously, "Before you take off I have a one more question. Is there any chance the Davis family men have any connection to the Klan?"

Brice prepared to rise as he added another thought. "Honestly, I don't believe so, but I have no evidence either way. But I'll tell you what. There's a local barber here in town you might find helpful, but I've heard he's blown town for a couple days. However, his fishing buddy, a Mick butcher that works just up the road from Herman Kamp, might be able to assist you in your inquiry. That Irish punk hears all, sees all, and tells all for a small price. So there's a good chance he'll know all the scuttle-butt on local vice, the Klan, and just about everything else there is to know about underground activity here in the city. I'm not even sure he's a member. But he's in the know on most of the underground stirrings of the metro."

"Where do I find him?" I asked.

"Well, when you leave here, just walk down to 12th Street, take a right and keep walking until you get to Kamp's butcher house. Go around to the west side and ask the dock boss for Punchy O'Brien and have a chat. You might find it informative. I do, from time to time, when a case requires that kind of delicate inquires and I have questions in that direction. Anyway, his Christian name is Danny Francis Joseph O'Brien. Drop in there. He may have some answers for you and tell him I sent you. Maybe, he'll give you some clarification or map points in the right direction," he said in a frank tone.

I nodded. "Maybe I'll drop by on him then."

We finished the remainder of our iced teas, spun in our café stools; stood up and shook hands as he stated, "Say goodbye to me, Lou."

"Goodbye, Brice," I replied. Jackson was going to be late for his appointment, but I had a feeling he liked gossiping about the social set.

When he had left, I walked back to the men's room. It was dim and deserted. The big square room had been papered with posters from old rodeos and cattle sales. I finished my business, exited and walked to the end of the counter. A brass cash register sat under the window where it stood guard duty over the Café exit.

A small-built brunette in her thirties stood behind the register. I handed two Lincolns to the tired-looking cashier; she rang me up, gave me a forced smile as she handed me my change. I pushed an ace back over the counter and told her; "Give this to Mabel." She took it while she wound one of her brown curls up on the back of her neck and watched me turn and walk out the door.

Chapter Eight

Outside of the lunch box the sky was red, and it was the start of another muggy afternoon. I walked along Agnew, watching the cowboys drive longhorns down the street towards the yards. The sweet smell of money rose up from the manure piles left atop the cobbled street into my nostrils, it burned slightly. I turned off the street and Kamp's Meat Company butcher house rose up before me. There was a lot action going on. Two small delivery trucks were backed up to the building where men in white butcher coats, capes and paper hats were loading one truck and unloading the other. I walked around to the west side and went in.

Three men were cutting meat on chopping blocks, while crates of dead chickens were stacked and dripping with melting ice. Legs of lambs were hanging from wall hooks. There was a bloody hunk of some kind of meat on a scale hung from the ceiling, and through a window in a room-size icebox I saw another butcher making mountains of chopped meat at a grinder. A slopped-faced joker left one of the blocks, a big knife still in his mitt, and asked in a Swedish accent, "Yeah, mister?"

"Is Danny O'Brien around?"

"He's out in the market, but he should be back in a few minutes."

"I'll wait."

He didn't ask me who I was, merely went back to work. I found a chair and sat. There were a number of large wicker baskets against one wall, each with a bar or eating place tagged on the handle. I gathered they supplied meats to these numerous places as well as their own deli I knew they ran on Classen.

The butchers were filing orders; slopped-face weighed up a steak, wrapped it and tossed it into one of the baskets, and checked it off on an order pad. Then he went into the icebox and came out with a whole liverwurst, a bag of franks, and chopped meat.

In the other baskets I could see tins of frozen livers, turkeys, loins of pork, and other meats. There were three phones, and they seemed to be working all the time. There was a kind of office at one end of the store, and some old guy who looked like a bookkeeper answered the phone and then called out. "Jake, Owl Café wants a fresh ham. How much?"

A butcher working with a pocked-marked face yelled back, "Forty-nine cents a pound."

The bookkeeper told the guy on the other end of the phone and there was a sort of argument and the bookkeeper put the phone and called out, "Jake, talk to the Owl."

Jake dropped a cleaver and picked up one of the phones, said, "Kurt? Yeah, yeah, that's right, forty-nine cents a pound. So what are you fighting with me for? Pork is sky high on the market. Don't have no hams. Look, we got some canned picnics from Holland you can have for twenty-five cents a pound. What? Kurt, you want a ham or not? I'm busy. Okay, okay, they run about twelve pounds. What else you want? How much chopped meat? Sure it's all lean, you know us."

Next to the icebox there was another room-sized freezer. Every few minutes one of the butchers would dash in and a foggy ice vapor would come out. Soon as he opened the door a light went on and I saw shelves with frozen turkeys, chickens, and meats. Everything wrapped in some kind of bag.

I was sitting there about ten minutes when a stocky young man carrying a half a cow, or something, on his shoulder waltzed in. He was wearing a white butcher coat, caked with blood in varying degrees of dryness, but no hat, and he had thick bushy red hair. He hung the meat on a hook, and pock-face jerked his thumb at me and the kid came over and asked, "What's the rumpus, mister?"

"I just need a few moments of your time." I stated as I stuck out my hand.

"My names Lou Nayland."

"Cop?" His Irish-gray eyes harden a trifle.

I nodded no. Whereby he whipped his dirty hand on his coat and shook mine. "Danny O'Brien, pleased to t'meetcha, mate. What's your business?"

Taking out a cigarette and lighting it, I replied, "Private Dick. A mutual friend known for wearing a big Stetson suggested you might be able to help me out. Is there someplace we can speak in private?"

He nodded and pointed towards the door leading outside. When we both stood in the bright sun, I noticed the big Swede who I recognized played for the Indians carrying a whole cow on his back walking into another door. I nodded in his direction, "Do you know that guy?"

O'Brien mumbled, "Yeah, kind of."

"What's his name?" I inquired.

"Borgerson, I believe. He's one of those pro baseball players. There's four or five of them that work the docks when they have a couple of days off. Keeps them strong and they work cheap. But I did over hear one of them say they make more on the docks in two days than they make in a week playing ball." He returned to my initial question and asked. "What can I answer for you?"

Taking a drag, I explained that I was looking for information on the local Ku Klux Klan and who might possibly belong to such an organization.

The redhead leaned in and whispered, "That's not exactly something anyone talks about in daylight in these parts."

"I know, but can you help me out?"

"Wish I could, but to be frank, I don't know much about those dossers other than what I read in the paper."

"Nothing?"

"Nope, but I might know someone that does. Did our mutual friend mention a guy by the name of David Flatten?"

"He suggested that possibility to me, yes."

The young man went on, "He's a slabber with a shop on North Walker, but I heard he's out of town seeing his ma until Thursday of Friday. Probably best you wait and talk to him if you want to learn anything about the guys you were asking about. He'll know more about those characters then I could tell you." He extended his hand. "I've got to get back to work, but you go ask David for a bazzer and see what he tells ya." We shook hands as if we liked each other as I slipped him a couple of bucks before he walked back into the shop.

Chapter Nine

With three hundred dollars of inspiration in my pocket, the O'Brien lead a dead end and the Flatten guy apparently out of town, I headed toward my parked Ford. I got into the coupe, revved the engine and pulled a U-turn on Agnew, and pressed the car north toward Sixth Street.

During my lunch conversation with Sheriff Jackson, he let something slip about the Camp woman's husband without realizing the importance it could bear on the case. But I'd caught it and made a note. I decided that I should probably wander out to Holland Field and see the kid's boss, the Indians' manager, Bert Neihoff. Most coaches know the heads of their players better than their own wives'.

Neihoff and I were friends, mostly because he appreciated when I swung by for little impromptu bull sessions about the history and abilities of baseball and its players. He considered me the wisest, wittiest, and most interesting minor league ballplayer who didn't hail from the east coast. And of course, I was in complete accord with his evaluation.

We first met when I played for the Ft. Worth Cats, seventeen years ago. At the time, he started as second baseman for the St. Louis Cardinals. Back then, the major ball clubs traveled through the South, playing minor league teams as they returned home to start their seasons. I had had the fortune or misfortune to play against Bert in one of these exhibition games in the spring of '19.

Neihoff's first time at bat that day, he hit a Daisy Cutter into the hot corner of the field and strolled easily to first base where I was positioned. He immediately started working on my head with his unique chaff and banter.

"Relax, Kid, you can't stop me from stealing second."

"Just remember to catch the ball when your lame pitcher tries to pick me off."

Bert smiled. "You'll be fine."

"Try anything you want. I'm just along for the ride, but then again. I might put the hammer down on you," I replied as the old fox gave me a mischievous grin.

When Stiely started his next wind-up, Bert took off for a second like a bullet from a gun. It surprised our pitcher Stiely, making him throw out to me instead of Bancroft on second. By the time I caught the ball; Bert came out of his slide and waved back at me with a leer.

Bert kept his trash talk for the remainder of the game. Ty Cobb was renowned for his trash talk after that day. I would have bet Bert rivaled him. After the game, we stood on the field talking until the stadium cleared. We shared similar views on baseball as well as the world at large and stayed in contact for the remainder of the season. We joked often of our rematch in the up-coming spring.

Bert hung up his cleats that fall after playing only five seasons in the show. It's a mighty fine thing for a man to know when he's had enough.

The organization offered him a scouting job, combing the minor league clubs for prospects. He phoned me late in the following season to see if I might be interested in moving up the next spring to play in one of the Cardinal's farm teams. He hadn't heard of my injury. Several years later, we became re-acquainted when he took over as the skipper of the Oklahoma City Indians. I figured it was a good day to swap lies, argue about the team's prospects, politics and, hopefully, insight on his right fielder, Johnny the "Toad" Camp, both on and off the diamond.

I drove out to the ballpark on Penn, knowing the Indians didn't have a game scheduled for today and they'd finished their morning batting practice by now.

The August sun shone brightly off the advertisements painted across the exterior fence. I looked up as the empty press box swayed to-and-fro on its elevated posts in the stiff prairie summer wind. During game days the local CBS radio station KOMA 1520 broadcasted the Indians' home games across the regional southwest.

I walked to the first gate and pulled. It was locked, so I walked down the line, checking each, until I noticed the second to last had been left ajar. It left just enough of a gap for me to slip through. The turnstiles inside weren't locked down, so I pushed in.

Inside, the breeze was considerably less noticeable and the only things stirring were the spiders spinning silky webs between the support beams of the bleachers. The best seats in the place were behind home plate, which was protected from the sun by a tar roof. The segregated seats were set along the first baseline in the open air. Refreshment stands sat under the bleachers near the aisle stairs. The faint smell of buttered popcorn reached my nose as breeze circled through the stadium. *God, I love ballparks!*

A voice behind me brought me back to reality. "Something I can do for you?"

It was Putter, the aging head grounds keeper who maintained Holland Field as the best-kept diamond in the Texas League. I stuck my right hand out to shake, "I'm here to see Coach Neihoff." We met several times before, but he always seemed to forget who I was.

I introduced myself again. "I'm Lou Nayland."

Putter looked over his wire-framed glasses and replied. "Oh yeah, I didn't recognize you at first. You're that private dick that played for the Cats down in Texas years back, I recall. If you're looking for Bert, I think he's still in his office down by the locker room."

Putter removed his canvas glove, and we shook hands. "The field looks great and I see you got a couple new city rats to help you this summer."

"Thanks, and I better get down to the field with them. I'm way behind already." He said as he headed to the field.

I strode towards the stairs that led to the locker rooms and dugout. Out of the corner of my eye I read the local advertisements plastered on the outfield fence; Cain's Coffee, Simpson's Ford, and W.L. Buck Sporting Goods. I continued on down the stairs.

The damp and grubby hallway ran for fifty feet. Water dripped from overhead pipes. I followed the pipes until I reached a smoked glass door. That read LOCKER ROOM, PLAYERS ONLY in green lettering. I knocked on the oak framed door.

From inside came a gruff booming voice, "Yeah, what do you want?"

"Coach, it's Lou Nayland, you got a few minutes to gab?"

"Sure, come on in."

I stepped into the most cluttered, dog-box office I had ever seen. I let the door close behind me.

Bert sat in a swivel chair wearing last season's Indians uniform. The coach had a square jaw and large ears protruding out at right angles from his head. They made his melon appear larger than it actually was. His shoulders were wide enough to yoke a pair of oxen. The front page of the *Daily Oklahoman* sports section was spread across the top of the desk. Pinned to the wall were scouting reports of the various Texas League teams with notes in red, written in the margins.

"How the hell are you, Lou?" he said as he stood up and shook my hand. He still maintained a batters grip.

"Good," I replied, still searching the room for something to sit on. Other than Bert's chair, the only seat available was a four foot long bench with PROPERTY OF THE INDIANS stenciled across the top. I straddled it, facing Bert.

Smirking, he asked, "You still make a living peeping into keyholes and following middle-aged cheaters around?"

"Mostly, but I try to crawl up from the gutters once in a while. I've been above ground enough to know your boys are tearing the league up."

"Yeah, I'm real proud of the fellas this season. Evans has been tops pitching and our lineup batted well through July. You catch any of the games?"

"As a matter of fact, I caught that victory over Galveston on Friday or whatever day it was. The team sure looks strong. They held off the Buc's late surge, and The Toad ended it with a great catch."

"I thought so. What can I do for you today?"

"Nothing in particular, baseball mostly, you know, just looking for your insight on my day off."

He growled, "Don't kid me. I'm too old and tired and, besides, I can see from the way you're kicking the dirt that you have something specific on your mind, so let's have it."

"I kind of hate to mix my business with our friendship, but something I've been looking into, a domestic situation, may or may not have an effect on one of your players."

Bert leaned back. "That's a hell of a way to start a conversation. It's surely not the kind of inquiry a manager cares to have pop up during a winning season."

I let the brush-back go by. "It's not the kind of thing I like talking to you about. To be honest, I would rather talk about averages and pennant races."

Bert picked up a worn baseball from the desk and tossed it back and forth between his hands, asking, "Whose sidecar thinks her man is stepping out on the town?"

I stalled a few moments and then replied, "Johnny Camp's wife."

His eyes blazed wide. "I'm not happy to hear that name, but you never know about the quiet ones, do you?"

Bert squeezed the baseball in his left hand. "Damn, I wish all my boys would keep their privates out of the holiest of the holies until the season's over. You know I'll help you if I can, but you got to keep what I say under your ball cap. I can't afford to have locker-room distractions this late in the season. God damn it, we're playing too damn HOT! And I don't need some damn Annie, or even a wife for that matter, muckin' up my season."

"Without a doubt," I stated calmly. "So what can you tell me about the kid you have playing right field?"

I heard faint footsteps just outside the door. Figuring it must have been some players leaving the clubhouse, I waited for him to respond.

Bert placed the baseball down and reached for a cigarette from the pack lying on his desk. It was empty, so I took a fresh pack of Camels from my coat pocket and tossed it on his desk. Bert picked them up, removed a stick and began rolling it back and forth between his strong fingers so that tobacco spilled out of both ends.

"The Toad? He's a good kid. You know the type, right off the farm and wet behind the ears. Baseball wise, he's in his second season here after the club picked him up off a sandlot team in Borger, Texas. Off the field he mostly keeps to himself, is soft spoken and kind of a hayseed, but he's hardworking and his teammates like him. They all tend to look after him on the road."

I leaned back on the bench, scratched at the two days' growth on my face, a nervous tick I had developed since becoming a PI and looked down. "That's all fascinating if I were in the numbers game, but maybe I should be more specific. What do you know about his wife? Does she, or has she caused him any trouble this season?"

Bert sighed. "Like I said, he got here early last season, April sometime, to start workouts. He worked hard and kept to himself. But you know as well as I do that there's always a flock of local Annies hovering around the ballpark, and at first they all took to his boyish looks and his soft-spoken manner. You know me, I run them off as best as I can, but Annies don't discourage easily."

I nodded in agreement as he continued, "Anyway, about three weeks into the season, a sleek tall blonde started hanging around with the young players. I could tell right off that she wasn't your usual Okie gal, especially after I overheard her working her angle on some of the boys. Brother, she ain't no Okie."

"Yeah, I've met her," I said. "She may live here, but her heart's not from here."

Bert shook his head in confirmation. "She reminded me of those society dames from back East trying to cover up her southwest twang."

He tossed the ball into the air again. "In any case she soon had a bead on The Toad. She made an effort to chew gum with him every day after practice."

Bert spun the ball on his desk. "After a while I stopped bothering about it because it didn't seem to have much effect on the kid's game. Matter of fact, she appeared to give him more confidence, so I let it slide. By June he had fallen hard and she had her hooks in deep."

The coach continued with his one ball juggling act, "The kid's no cake-eater, so there was no stopping the train. He was putty in her hands, and by August they married. Anyhow, as far as I can tell, they have been happy blessed newlyweds ever since."

"Malarkey, Coach," I blurted out. "That's a great story for *Sporting News*. Now, you wanna give the Neihoff extra innings report?"

Bert flushed as I continued, "You're with these boys day and night and you hear their chatter and I know for a fact that you have a spy in the player's wives' box. You try to screen the crap that comes out of there before it reaches the clubhouse."

He nodded as I continued. "We both know all too well they chirp their way through the entire game and those little songs filter into the locker room through their husbands. I'm guessing that an outsider that looks like the Camp dame puts a bee in their bonnets, making her a prime target for all their gossip."

Bert gave me a knowing smile as I said, "I've met her. She could overturn the hen house with her looks alone. To make it worse, she's not the ice-cream social type. Her temper can flare as red as her nails and then become as cold as a butchers ice box in the next. So let's be honest. Even you don't believe that candy-coated love story crap you just spilled."

A large grin formed on Bert's face. It was the type of look all great storytellers seemed to sport when it's a tasty tale. "I'm not sure what you're getting at," he said, trying to throw me off.

"Coach, you know these guys inside and out. Knock the dirt off your cleats and give me the lowdown. I'm trying to help them out. I'm not here to cause trouble for your boy, but trouble might be coming for him. So I'll ask it another way. Is there something about him, her, or both, that might be embarrassing if brought out into the light of day?"

"That's hard to say. Because, you see, I don't know anything in particular about the woman or her habits."

He took another drag off his smoldering cigarette. "But you know locker rooms. They're very small communities with very few secrets. So it's not too difficult to overhear a filthy joke or two. Truthfully, earlier this season I heard a few dirty comments directed at The Toad."

He paused as if expecting a question from me, but getting none plunged on. "Most of what I heard seemed a little farfetched for such a nice young couple. You know me. I just took the tales as guys chiding one another in the locker room and blew it off as juvenile nonsense. Besides his pals, the big Swede and the kid from Jersey shut it down pretty quickly."

I leaned forward and said, "I'm glad he has some cover, but I need to know what the chatter was about if I'm going to help out the kid."

Bert crushed out the cigarette in a tin tray. "You're kind of putting me in a pickle here, Lou. Frankly, I hate to repeat locker room banter. You know as well as I do that it's an unspoken rule, nothing said inside the clubhouse goes out the door."

"Coach, I still feel like I'm part of the locker room fraternity and I surely don't want to jinx the team's streak, so if it's best left unsaid, we can just leave it here on the floor and we'll talk more baseball. You know, for you, I'll head any trouble off I can before it affects you or the locker room."

Bert nodded in appreciation. "Besides, I would like to help you out if I can and especially if, in the process, it helps my client. So like I said, I still feel bound to the fraternity. Why don't you just spell it out and maybe we both can head off any future annoyances?"

"Damn, honestly, Lou, the rumors seem too unnatural and cruel for me to think possible, but if you've been hired by the wife to keep them both out of harm's way I'll trust you to keep trouble from our door as well."

"Coach, you know I will."

"But still, it's some weird shit," he said, shaking his head.

I bent forward, "Okay, Coach, shock me. You're no rube, so now I'm curious what a man of a thousand dugouts considers to be unnatural and weird."

Bert reached across the desk and grabbed his red lead pencil and rolled it around the inside of his ear. "How do I put this? When you were stationed in France during the war did you ever hear about those Frog husbands who liked to watch their wives perform in the brothels?"

That stopped me dead. "I guess I ran with a quieter crowd over there than I thought. Because I'm a little foggy on how's that connected to the Camp's current situation?"

Bert turned away, looked down at the sports page lying on his desk, continuing to turn the pencil around in his ear. "God damn it, Lou, you're not that much of a hayseed. You damn well know what I mean. He's one of those guys who likes to watch his wife screw other guys."

"You're right, Coach, it's a little unnatural. If true, contrary to popular belief, it's proof that there is something new under the sun for some of us. Look, I'll do everything I can to shield the club if the case that I'm on and what you just told me are connected and I'm able to protect my client's interests. Next time, let's just talk baseball."

We both stood and shook hands. I walked to the door and turned back. "Thanks for your insight."

As I left the coach's office I nearly crashed into two ballplayers. Both wore baseball pants, no shirts, and towels wrapped around their necks. They had abs cut so deep they looked like newly rolled steel rods piled atop of each other. Sweat droplets formed across their large barrel chests. One was six inches taller than the other, with shoulders wider than the door. He appeared distinctly Nordic looking, with Viking blonde hair atop a sun-bronzed face, chiseled jaw and arctic blue eyes that were focused on me.

His partner gave me a large smile below a well-groomed mustache that matched the prodigious amount of black curly hair on his head and naked torso.

They both appeared to be on a mission. The big Swede put his muscular hand atop my shoulder, stopping me dead in my tracks. The darker one spoke to me in a distinct New Jersey accent. "Shamus, you're making a real brodie comin' out here today and sticking your schnoz in where it doesn't belong. I suggest it would be in your best interest to lay off Johnny and just forget any stories you've heard."

I wished I had tucked my sap into my coat pocket that morning, but at the time, I hadn't thought that looking into Mrs. Camp's problem necessitated such a solution. I quipped, "Boys, I think you're just bumping gums. Now why don't you kids go shag some fly balls and get out of my way?"

Jersey Boy retorted, "I think we've caught all the fly balls we need today,

Shamus. The more important question is, what's a key-hole peeper like you doing sneakin' around where decent people are earning a dime?"

"Hey, guys, I'm just a retired Texas leaguer catching up with the skipper and congratulating him on your season."

Jersey Boy scowled at me. "For your sake, I hope you're here to get the background reports from the coach, but I got a feeling you're here just to cause trouble and you're snowin' us, Shamus. Either way, it's time for you to scram or I'm going to bend you into a jug handle like on Route 9."

His pal, the big Swede, nodded and mumbled something incoherent. A confrontation wasn't what I needed, especially since I'd just promised Bert that I wouldn't allow his locker room to be tainted. Now these two dim-wits could accidentally do just that. I took a step towards the big Swede, hoping to get around.

The Swede spoke languidly. "Maybe we're not finished yet."

I heard a laugh over my right shoulder, I turned, looked at the Jersey Boy, but that was a mistake. I didn't see the first blow coming. But I felt it land as the Swede cold-cocked my unprotected jaw. With an almost audible gust, the saliva rolled into my mouth. The pain of a good punch always starts with nausea down deep within one's gut, not at the point of impact. I went over sideways, but attempted to spread my legs to absorb the wallop and stay standing. It was mistimed, and I tripped, causing my body to nose dive. My head was not as hard as the concrete wall it smashed into. For a brief, blurred minute, I saw Jersey Boy sneering down at me in triumph as he spoke.

"Are you going to lay off the Camps, Shamus?"

Through fading light, I looked back at Jersey Boy and mumbled as the darkness rolled over me. "Did Jesus stop making furniture just because the Romans beat him up?"

"Abyssinia, Shamus." And out I went.

When I came to, I felt cold and sweaty and had a headache a yard wide. The bright light of a medical flashlight burned into my eyes and smelling salts scorched my nose. I blinked a few times and twisted around. Through blurred vision I made out Pepper, the Indians' trainer. He continued to look into my eyes with his light blinding me, but he pulled the salts away from my face.

I heard Bert ask, "You alright, Lou? What happened?"

"I'm fine, *mon capitaine,* merely a flesh wound." But my head hurt worse than a homebrew hangover. I felt sticky blood roll down my cheek, but my jaw appeared no worse for wear. I suspected the newly forming bruise where the big Swede hit me wouldn't be as severe as the cut received from the cement wall. I tried to stand up. I didn't make it. "If only some Florence Nightingale would attend to me properly, my recovery would be complete."

Shaking his head, Pepper kneeled down and attempted to stop the bleeding from the weeping wound with a training towel soaked in alcohol.

"Ouch!"

The smell of the tonic and the rising headache made my stomach turn. I used my right arm to lever myself up, and managed to get into a sitting position, weaving back and forth several times as I continued up onto my knees and tried to maintain an upright position. When I'd done so I went through my pockets. Nothing appeared gone. A few minutes later, I knew I was going to make it.

"This will settle the wasps in your belly," Pepper said. I took the bottle of Old Bean he held in his out-stretched hand and took a swig. The haze around the corners of my eyes cleared.

"Guess I wasn't paying attention and tripped on the top step."

Not wanting to involve the two ball players until I knew more of the whys, I said nothing. For all I knew, they were just two overly concerned pals of The Toad, doing what they thought was right. Teammates having a friend's back.

The Swede and Jersey kid hadn't hung around. Bert and Pepper just stood there looking at me, probably suspecting I still carried a hangover around from the night before.

"I'm copacetic, thanks for the talk, Coach, good luck tomorrow." I strode off toward the stairs and yelled back, "Hey, Coach, don't take any wooden nickels until you win the pennant."

As I left the stadium, I knew my legwork hadn't gone exactly as planned, but it hadn't been a total trip for biscuits. I'd picked a few crumbs from the plate.

I headed towards 21st Street to see a friend. I needed to step away from my day, reset the mental tumblers, and consider other avenues of attack in my attempts to resolve the Camp matter.

Chapter Ten

Steering the car east along 4th Street, I weaved through the slow-moving afternoon traffic towards the State Capital district. Driving with my head held out the open car window, I attempted to clear my mind by catching the stiff breeze blowing into the little coupe.

I'd decided after my short workout at the ballpark with The Toad's friends I could use a stiff drink, some pleasant conversation, a square meal, and a brief reprise from the vigor of my investigation. The best place to satisfy all those needs was at my friend Irene's establishment.

I dropped into a little underground dive that sold untaxed liquor and picked up a bottle of a good rye, Irene's drink of choice. It had been my practice when popping in to bring a bottle to smooth my unexpected entrance into her home.

Nearing Irene's neighborhood, I could just make out the lights atop the huge oil derricks laboring away, pumping oil from the field that sits under the State Capital several blocks east of her place on Lincoln Boulevard.

Irene had transformed her home on Olie Avenue into a boarding-house after her husband left. She currently rented out the four bedrooms located on the second floor in a valiant attempt to keep the wolves from her door. Queerly his leaving her was due to the fact he was currently doing a three to five stretch for an embezzlement rap down in "Big Mac," the state pen in McAlester. Unfortunately, and for good or bad, I had had a lot to do with his current state of incarnation.

Roughly a year back, I'd taken an investigative job with the Piggly-Wiggly grocery store on 10th Street to determine why the owner's monthly books hadn't balance of late. The snoop job uncovered that the store's butcher, Irene's husband Fred, was selling prime cuts of beef out the back door and pocketing the money. During his five day trial, I made myself acquainted with his country gold of a wife with the penetrating brown eyes.

After a couple sweltering afternoons in the hall of the old courthouse, I concluded she was aces. She was the type of bird who had to think twice about giving you the time of day and then would probably give you a bum steer when she did. I liked her instantly. Over the course of her husband's trial, she developed a small torch for me as well. After Judge Lucius Babbcock sentenced Fred up the river, we spoke for some time in the hall.

"He must be guilty. Twelve good men found him guilty," she said stoutly on the day of her husband's sentencing when the sheriff's deputies walked him in cuffs past us in the corridor of the eighth floor. As he disappeared into the jail elevator, she noted that four of the twelve jurors had been women and should have at least shown some consideration for her situation in the matter.

Since then I had, from time to time, dropped in on Irene to make sure she wasn't getting lonely. She slept in the back-room on the first floor of her two-story boarding house. She charged her boarders $1.25 a day for a clean bed; a home-style breakfast every morning and a hearty dinner at 6:30 pm if the tenant appeared bathed and timely at her table.

I knew she currently had only one boarder in residence. Sean, a red-headed Irish youth who held a job as a linesman for the Topeka run of the Atchison, Topeka and Santa Fe railway line. He's route only ran on Monday and Thursday evenings. Which meant Sean would be away for twenty-four hours stretches on those evenings. Coincidently, for some strange reason those tended to be the evenings I ended up on Irene's front porch.

On one particular Thursday night, I happened to drop in for a hot meal and conversation. Sean, whose Atchison run was delayed, enthusiastically joined us for dinner. As we waited for Irene to serve the meal, he attempted to speak to me with a series of sophomoric questions about what it took to be a private detective.

I gave him the usual answers. It was best if he did a couple years with the police department. He asked if there were quicker ways to achieve that position, explaining he had recently come to a decision to become a cinder dick for the railroad. Like all young men, he wanted a shortcut to his dream. Luckily, I hadn't bumped into him since.

My thoughts trailed off like smoke as I quit watching the laboring derricks, slowed the coupe and made a wide arching turn onto Olie. The street was a concrete paved road that sloped gently towards Irene's house situated on the southeast corner of 21st Street. As I passed the 15 MPH speed sign, I pulled in and parked my car parallel to Irene's house. I grabbed the bottle of rye while exiting the Ford and strode up to the front door.

Irene's house didn't stand out on the street, being a typical wood clabbered job with asymmetrical facades, large front gables and overhanging eaves. A large porch covered the right half of the frontage providing shade and kept the lower part of the house cool in the sizzling Oklahoma summers.

A large liver-ticked dog came out from under the porch and squared himself between me and the front door, and growled. It was Irene's dog, Patches. Being somewhat of an intimidating creature, I smoothly closed the distance between us as I slowly reached down and stroked the mutt behind his large floppy brown ears. We were now friends.

Looking up, I noticed Irene leaning against the railing of the second-floor balcony, beating a hall runner with a wired carpet cleaner. The dog and I continued to be partners watching Irene swat the fray-edged weaved rug. Little rivers of sweat glistened in the sizzling summer sun as they rolled slowly down her beautifully bronze-chest between two perfectly formed dirty pillows. Several locks of her silky brunette hair had fallen out from under the tightly wrapped, blue kerchief stuck to her damp forehead.

Her exertion formed two large, darkly stained marks under both of her arms. I stood there, appreciating her prairie wife, rugged good looks. She still maintained the long, tight form of the young, even though her chassis had broadened slightly over the years. Contrary to the thoughts of young men, it had only enhanced her sexuality, making her more striking and desirable looking. I was tough, but Irene was tougher. She was about the toughest dame I ever knew. She knew what she had, and her only aim in life was to make it pay off for her.

I stood there admiring her curved feminine form, as I did so she glanced down at me with a twinkle of a smile. Her grin caused her cheek bones to pull up and out, causing her roan colored shutters to brighten behind her wire-framed cheaters. It had been a while since I had made a genuine smile come across a woman's face. I wanted to see it some more.

She looked down at me. "Well, look what the cat's drug up onto my front porch. How is it with you, Lou?"

"Everything is Jake, Angel. Care to split a bottle of rye and wait for the stars to come out?"

"That's the best idea I've heard in a long time. I'll be right down, so why don't you come on in and sit in my parlor." She stated with a dash of playfulness and a wink.

In answer to her drawled "Come on in," I took the front steps two at a time onto the porch, turned the brass knob on the newly painted red front door and walked on in. I stopped briefly in the foyer, catching sight of the large country style dining table with wild flowers set in the middle in a jelly jar. It had eight ladder-back chairs pushed in evenly around its edges. Behind the table was a set of swinging wooden doors that led to the kitchen at the rear of the house. Directly across from the front door, a beautiful carved staircase with ornate hand carved rails climbed up to the second-story bedrooms.

I half-whirled into the front room, pushing open the two sliding, stained glass panel doors. The room had a green-tiled fireplace below a wooden mantle, as well as two brown woven Queen Anne chairs, turned slightly to fit into the alcove of the curved bay windows that faced the front yard. A matching brown woven couch sat to the right of the fireplace facing the high-back chairs. Other than a cracked oblong mirror over the fireplace, the walls were bare.

The window curtains appeared faded to white, but if you looked carefully, they still retained the faint hue of the original yellow dye. The rooms and the house stood like a grand old lady who had faded over time. It spoke of a family once having wealth, but I had never asked Irene about it. The money was long gone and the house now represented the current depression

72

engulfing the country.

I entered the room, sat on the edge of the couch placing the brown paper bag containing the bottle of rye and my fedora on the pine coffee table that hovered above my out-stretched legs.

Irene entered through the stained glass paneled doors. She had discarded her blue handkerchief and brushed her luxurious brunette hair back, allowing it to flow over her shoulders. She now wore a wine colored print dress with a small white belt tied about her waist that showed off her curves without bragging about them. Irene glided across the floor as she ran her long slender fingers through her hair one more time, attempting to smooth the sweat curls that had formed while she had worked. With the grace only a confident woman can pull off, she continued her dancing and swirled across the huge front room, while asking me how I liked her new dress.

Without looking up at her I said, "I think it looks wonderful on you."

Irene continued her graceful gestures around the room, as she explained that the color was red burgundy and that the dinguses on the side were something or other.

I sat, taking her and the dress in, while I smirked at her blatant attempt at seduction. "You look fantastic."

"You really think I look good in it?" Her somber eyes fastened themselves on me, intent and warm.

"You always look good, doll," I said with my most playful smile, then excitedly added, "the Indians are in the race for first place in the Texas League this week."

She made a face at me and said, "You don't give a damn about my dress." She said it in jest, or at least, I hoped she did.

Irene gazed at me with her sullen brown eyes and smiled a toothy grin, her teeth glistening white as she did so. My minor indiscretion had been forgiven. She sat down on my lap, gently crossing her legs as she reached over and gave me a peck on the cheek. The kiss almost made me blush because of its warmth and delicacy. It felt swell having Irene on my lap, smelling her, talking to her.

Pushing Irene off my lap, I reached into my coat pocket and retrieved a pack of smokes. Withdrew two and placed them between my lips, removed a silver lighter from my pants pocket and lit them both then handing one to Irene. She placed it softly between her recently applied, red stained lips, took a long draw, and let the smoke escape perfectly out of her mouth into small gray circles lifting skyward as she kept her eyes on me the whole time.

"What's happened to you today, love? You have a cut that's bleeding all over my couch from the side of your head, and it looks deep, too," she stated with mild concern as she reached out to inspect the wound over my ear.

"Oh, just a little misunderstanding, you know my usual kind of day."

She stood and walked to the worn side board in the corner, removed two tumblers, returned to the couch and placed them before us. I took out the bottle of hooch and filled each glass three fingers deep. Irene looked at me with voluptuously red lips, gave me a kiss on the forehead before rising and picking up the two glasses from the table, and walking out the way she had originally come in.

I heard her Cuban-heeled oxfords click on the wood floor as she walked toward the back of the house. The clicking noise stopped as the sound of the squeaky kitchen door swinging back and forth trailed down the hall.

A few moments later, the renewed click of the heels resonated in such a pitch to indicate her return. Irene appeared through the sliding doors holding the glasses filled with chunked ice and what appeared to be a damp kitchen rag. She sat again, handed me one of the cool glasses and took a dainty sip of hers, set it down and pressed the cool wet rag onto the side of my battered head. "Better?"

I nodded as she asked, "So, if you won't give me the details of how you got yourself cut today, what should we talk about?"

After removing my suit coat, I leaned back into the corner of the couch and told her my little story of Mrs. Camp. After thirty minutes we had exhausted the subject and she excused herself to fix us something to eat.

I was expected to dine at the table and be scrubbed. Therefore, I did and was. Irene definitely knew how to feed a man. Dinner consisted of the most delicious homemade meatloaf I'd ever had, along with a steaming pot of green beans cooked with fat back. In no time at all, we had finished both the meal and half the bottle of rye.

She went out to the kitchen and returned with a serving of cream covered peaches. After we'd devoured dessert, Irene sprang up and placed her oval framed glasses on the dining room table, dancing a samba like performance the length of the table while displaying a playful girlish smile upon her lips. She swirled on her final step ending up behind me, the move being pre-planned. While doing so, she intentionally brushed my shoulder with her breasts at the same time she ran her tender hand up from my wrist to the back of my ear. Synchronously Irene leaned over and placed several honey coolers on the sides of my neck. I caught the faint sweetish odor of flowers as I noticed the tiny gold locket, which had belonged to her mother, dangling below her throat as it rose and fell with each gasp of her shallow breath.

The warm, moist contact of her lips upon my skin was the only invitation I needed. "I don't like to be manhandled," I stated playfully. "Not even by beautiful women who resemble Greek goddesses."

Irene took my hand and led me back to her small, dark, cool bedroom at the northwest corner of the house. She slipped out of her wine colored dress, revealing only a white body slip. Irene threw her dress over a chair and walked back to the kitchen. Shortly, she returned carrying a speckled red tin pan containing a large chunk of block ice. I unlaced my shoes, kicked them off, and reclined back onto the bed as I watched her curiously place the ice on the corner table in front of a brass electrical fan. Reaching around the base, Irene hit the on/off switch causing the brass blades to begun to whirl. The flow of air from the blades blew her hair out in a sensual wave. She looked back at me and laughed.

Irene continued undressing as I studied the barely concealed swell of one perfect breast, the ivory mound of her lovely hips, the long, tapering lines of her beautiful legs. Upon finishing she crawled into bed next to me and declared, "Hello, handsome."

Waves of cool air generated from the melting ice and driven by the fan blades gradually reached the pair of us in bed. She shivered with her warm body next to mine. Feeling content, I took Irene into my arms and gave her the long desired kiss we both had anticipated all evening. As we separated she looked up into my eyes and ran her fingers through my chest hair. "Were you ever in love?" Her eyes were somber as she shyly asked.

I pulled her in closer as she flipped her hair at me. I inhaled her heavy perfume and the smell of sandal wood soap intoxicated me. Wrapped together I whispered, "I've never been married if that's what you're asking, but I had a girl when I was young in Fort Worth. Annie. She was an undergrad at Texas Christian University."

Irene scratched her nose pensively as I continued, "She was a tall, quiet gal with curly brunette hair who studied business. I might have even married her, but she ran off with a two-bit con man I was trying to nail on a check kiting scheme. Anyway, he was cornered in San Antonio by Texas Rangers and made a run for it, but a fast Santa Fe freight got in the way of his automobile." I hesitated, my voice catching in my throat. "Annie was in the car with him. Neither of them made it. Fort Worth wasn't the same after that, so I resigned from the force. Came north and hung my shingle out as a private detective. That was nearly ten years ago," I said in a dull tone.

Irene smiled up at me and said softly, "Sorry."

"Its old history and you make me happy now." I pulled her in closer. She closed her eyes and pushed her parted lips up until they met mine. She flicked her tongue at the tip of my nose, and said coyly, "That was sweet, Lou," then she kissed me hard. It was wet and passionate and we made love to one another until we both lay sweaty and exhausted. I faded off into a blissful sleep as my mind tried to determine whether it was Irene I had made love to or a faded memory of a youthful Annie.

Chapter Eleven

The following morning, the sound of my own breathing woke me from a deep slumber. I felt consumed with the sensation of being suffocated as my chest rose and fell with each attempted breath. It was as if there was no air in the room. But as the sensation seemed to become too overwhelming, I opened my eyes and realized I was drenched in sweat and my mouth tasting of cotton along with my pulse pounding in my head from the effects of the beating I'd received the day before.

Laying there, I ran my tongue over my gums as I took in the filtered light of the dawn. The sunlight oozed through Irene's ragged lace curtains, barely illuminating the room with a single dull, rusty color beam of light that spread across the far wall.

Slowly rolling my naked body over in the sweat soaked bed, I looked at the alarm clock on the nightstand. The dial read ten o'clock. I turned on the table radio and listened to some jazz. Patches, who'd been lying in the corner with his head on his paws, waiting for me to waken, whimpered and nuzzled my outstretched hand.

I suddenly felt someone watching me. Irene stood in the frame of the door. Her blue kerchief was tightly wrapped around her head. She had exchanged yesterday's dress for one of the lighter blue. She smiled at me. "You slept soundly last night. Hope it was because of me and not the rye. By the way, you slept right through another Black Roller that blew through town last night." "Black Roller" was a term to describe the huge dust storms that formed out west in the panhandle and if the wind was right, covered the city with red dust.

She walked around the room, picking up clothes as she talked. "The radio said it was worse than the Big One we had last April. You remember that one. That 'Roller' that carried all that red dust up towards New York City, causing the snow to fall red on those damn Yankees." She headed toward the kitchen.

That particular storm had been so severe it had reduced visibility around the state to less than ten yards. The storm engulfed every living thing in the western half of the state, killing many who failed to find shelter when the fine red dust overwhelmed their mouths and lungs, causing a slow, painful death by suffocation.

I called to Irene in the kitchen. "Can I still have breakfast?"

Irene reappeared in the doorway. "Breakfast? You're a little late on that, mister. But I'll tell you what, if you'll give me an honest day's work around here today, I'll get you a couple of eggs and some fat-back, but you'll get nothing more till your chores are done."

After I had finished my eggs I said, "I haven't any razor and I'm afraid I look disreputable."

Irene turned. "You look fine for the tasks I have for you. You'll find some of Fred's old work clothes laid out on the end of the bed. Put them on and get to work, sweetie," she said with a fiendish grin.

On top of the clothes pile, Miss Irene had left me a list of chores. I hee-hawed to myself as I read it.

An inch of red dirt covered the porch, and small drifts of dust covered the lawn. Irene's collection of a half-dozen chickens talked to each other in the coop. None of them seemed inclined to come outside and investigate my appearance on the scene. I guessed the storm's effect would result in few eggs being produced for days. So I got to work on the backdoor, but I gradually became distracted by a large pile of red dirt in the middle of the yard. It appeared to have white and black bar-like feathers arising from the pile. I was still concentrating on the unusual mound of dust when Irene came out, marched to that very spot, reached down and pulled up a dead Plymouth Rock hen and asked, "How's chicken and dumplings sound for dinner?"

"Great," I replied.

"Good, because when you're done out there you can come in and pluck this bird."

We ate the chicken and dumplings early and finished the rye with the meal. When we finished and cleaned the dishes, Irene said I could stick around another night, but I declined. I wasn't sure her tenant would return, but, in truth, neither one of us wanted to get that comfortable together. I needed fresh clothes and a good night's sleep. Besides, I had to be back in court in the morning to give testimony on another divorce case. I hoped it would be a one-day affair because I planned to throw myself back into the camp case.

My watch showed half-past six. So I walked over to the telephone and called my answering service. The girl at the other end said Lauren hadn't left a message regarding her attempts to arrange an appropriate meet and greet with her family. I hung up the receiver. I went back to Irene in the dining room, kissed her and repeated that I had to get back to my place on account of my date in court in the morning. Irene and I kissed at the door.

Grinning as I slid in behind the tiller of my Ford, I thought, "There have been other girls before Irene. She's the first who never objected to my way of life. She never questions where I've been or who with, or when I'll return to her doorstep." As that warm thought fell away I decided I would venture into the Deuce for some sleuthing before I hit the hay.

Chapter Twelve

Twilight was blending into night—it is that period that the natives called dusk-dark as I walked into Ruby's Bar and Grill across the street from the Aldridge. I had only visited once, so no one should recognize me if I sat in the closed booths along the rear wall. The small crowd inside looked at me as I walked past the bar, across the dance floor where a five-piece colored orchestra was blowing out a tune to a booth. Sitting down, I looked over the deafening room just as one of the house girls quickly sat down opposite of me and remarked, "They don't like strangers."

Her violet eyes glowed in the dim light of the club. Her oval face, notwithstanding the tiredness around the eyes, had an intriguing aspect about it. In the half-light she seemed young and nice-looking rather than pretty. Her voice, although not strong or cultivated, was sweet. Her black marcelled hair was cut short, parted in a long line along the right side and combed back over her well-shaped head in a charming way. As she slid deeper into the booth, she took a deep breath, which made her breasts stand tight against her silk-blue cocktail dress.

She told me her name was Janeth and asked, "Got a light, handsome?"

"Sure," I growled as I lit her cigarette. "Now run along. I have my own troubles."

"Thanks, but why, because you're waiting for one of the other girls?"

"I'm just looking for a drink and some solace."

Janeth breathed deeply again and said in a hushed tone, "Well, will you buy me one and we can both sit her quietly?"

"No," I said, "I don't. I just want to sit here and do some thinking."

A waiter stuck his head in the booth and Janeth said, "Hey, Kurt, this guy don't want to buy me a drink."

"What's he want?" Kurt demanded. "Hold his own hand? Tell him he can do that outside."

I decided I didn't want to draw attention to myself and ruin any chance I might have to learn something. I decided I would be less conspicuous in the Deuce with a girl than without one, so I asked, "What you drinking, sweetheart?"

"A Bee's Knees," she replied.

"Anything else?" the waiter asked.

"I'll have a scotch and water and your absence would be nice," I replied.

"Happy to oblige," Kurt rumbled.

As he headed back to the bar ,I asked Janeth, "You got a thing going with that waiter?"

"What?"

"What was that look he gave you?"

"It's your imagination."

"Possibly, but is he your boyfriend or something? Because I don't want any trouble."

"Relax, he's not my type. But you are."

"You're warming my heart, sweetheart."

"It's a hot night, ain't it?"

I didn't respond. I was trying to figure out if I was wasting my time in this jazz joint and whether this girl might know anything that would be helpful.

She lit a cigarette and tossed the pack on the table between us as the waiter returned with our drinks. He looked at us both, shook his head and strode off.

"Come on, handsome, drink up."

I examined her drink. "What's in there besides a fruit salad?"

"It's a mixture of lemonade, orange juice, honey, and gin. I like the honey." Her violet eyes gazed at me.

"Sounds too sweet for my taste," I replied.

"Maybe so, but I've learned to like it working in this joint for six months," she said. "You know, other than cops, you're the first ofay I've seen in this joint." She raised her eyebrows innocently.

I looked at the drink the waiter brought me. It was overly watered down, even for a scotch and water. "Like I told you earlier, I'm just here to do some thinking while I listen to the music. But hey, I've had a good week and I'm packing the dough to show it. So let's talk and I'll keep buying us drinks… hey, you listening to me?"

"Yeah, you got a big roll and you want to have some fun with it. I like fun."

"So do I, sweetheart, but let's take it slow and chat some first."

"You're nice, very nice," Janeth said with a wink, then babbled on. "I've never known any ofays that liked jazz before, but if you do, you and me can dance a little, chin a little, drink a lot and see what develops."

I nodded and smiled as the music broke off and the waiter simultaneously stuck his head in the booth. "You ready for another drink, buddy? That ain't a park bench you're sitting on."

Janeth spoke up first, "I'll take another one."

"Another scotch, but no water this time," I said.

The waiter brought the drinks, and I swiftly swigged half of it down.

"You must have been drunker than I thought when you came in. No one could drink that straight and be sober," Janeth said.

"I like it." I grinned.

"Oh," she said. "You're one of those straight whiskey drinkers, huh?"

"I would love to buy you a whiskey. But I'd love it better if you kept quiet and let me ask you some questions."

"It's okay with me. I get paid by the drink."

"You know that yellow-pink water will rot your stomach out," I said.

The band was blowing so loud it shook me in the booth. So I decided to ask the working twist what she knew about people in the club scene in the Deuce. But before I could begin, the waiter stuck his head in and looked at the empty glasses, and then at me with some new respect. He said, "Okay man, you want another round?"

"Scotch straight for me and another Bee's Knees for the lady, thanks."

Janeth spoke brusquely, "When you make mine this time, put two shots of liquor in my water. I gotta have something to help me stand up under this guy's conversation."

Kurt brought the drinks back and put mine gently on the table. "I'll bring water with the next one," he said. The guy underestimated me.

"You don't have to worry as long as I stick to scotch," I said. "I always stick to scotch when I drink fairly steady." It was sort of a bluff because the scotch was starting to hit me. I slowed to sipping the drink now before me.

"I've been drinking this yellow water a long time, but I ain't totally sold on it yet, other than the taste of honey on my lips."

"Won't they let you drink anything else?" I asked in a reasonable tone.

"Yeah, as long as I get the customer to buy it, but this is almost all pure profit and I get a bigger cut off one of these than off something that costs more. Besides, you can drink these all night."

That reminded me that I couldn't sit here all night talking and not gaining anything. So I decided to push Janeth on what she might know.

"Do you know many of the regulars down here?"

"Yeah, most of them. But no ofays, though. I do see some white gals come around the club."

"Do you know any of them?"

"Naw, but I've seen a few at the Aldridge on my nights off and when the Blue Devils are playing."

"Any of the white gals regulars?"

"No, not really, except there is one tall lanky blonde that comes down only when the Blue Devils are playing, but I've never met her nor do I know her name."

"Does she come in with anyone?"

"Not that I've seen. But I doubt she would because the word on the street is she's fooling around with one of the musicians, but I couldn't tell which one," she said.

Kurt stuck his head in. I was still sipping my drink. Janeth's glass was empty, so I ordered her another. "You ever heard anything about any of the musicians at the Aldridge messing around with any white gals?"

"No, the Christian brothers run a pretty tight ship. The only place I have ever seen the band is in the club or on their way to crash at the Littlepage. They travel a fair amount to Kansas City, so they don't mess with the locals much other than to play and get paid."

Kurt returned with the girl's drink and I asked for the check. He frowned and returned to the bar. Figuring I was no longer looking less conspicuous, I paid the check with a tip on his return.

I yawned. "Sorry, sister, I wish I wasn't so busy. I'd like to give you more of my time on the floor and chinning. You're a beauty, but I've got other business tonight. I'll stop in soon and we'll do this up right next time."

Janeth thanked me for the drinks and slithered out of the booth. Mumbling a curse, she began searching for her next payday.

I got up and quietly left the bar as the band started blowing again. As I let the door close behind me, I thought it might be best if I come back tomorrow during daylight hours before questioning anyone else in the Deuce.

Chapter Thirteen

I hit the sidewalk toward my parked coupe. The air was heavier than earlier. The electric threat of a summer storm was brewing in the sky beyond Packing-Town. I walked quicker, trying to recall everything I had learned to this point. It was a dismal list. The coming rain meant a cool night and a better night's sleep.

As I passed the Victoria Hotel, two bulky figures emerged from the shadows. Their features were obscured by the heavy hoods of their jackets. The pair each wore woolen newsboy caps. The front man had brass knuckles glinting from his fist, a knife gleamed in the hand of the second.

I backed up against the wall of the hotel in an attempt to shrink my body in on itself to make a smaller target. I tried to hide the fear forming in my eyes by swiveling my head from side to side and to keep both men in my view. I stuck my hands out as if to ward off an attack. I had trouble getting words past my closed-downed larynx.

"Christ, guys, I don't want any trouble. I'll give you everything I got. You don't have to hurt me."

The lead man laughed in a tone of triumph.

"A snoop, and a yellow-livered snoop besides. You've been sticking your nose into the wrong guys's business."

He swung the brass knuckles gripped in his hand at my head, but I'd already charged inside the arc of his swing and jammed my right elbow into his exposed throat.

His charge was so sudden that the second man's knife only cut through my jacket sleeve as I drove forward off my hind foot.

The top of my head crunched into Brass Knuck's chin. The man went backwards with blood spouting from his mouth as he gasped and choked before hitting the pavement with the back of his head. He lay motionless.

I whirled and drove my cupped hands simultaneously against both of the knifeman's ears. He howled with pain from the resulting shattering of his eardrums, landed on his knees, tipped over sideways, and laid still, clutching both sides of his head, grunting.

I looked quickly around. No pedestrians in sight. No traffic flowed on the street. Bending down over each man in turn, pulling back their hoods so I could see their faces. I didn't recognize either of them other than noting they were both colored men. I searched their pockets. No money, no I.D. I strode off toward my car.

My hands shook as I attempted to start the coupe. When she started, I drove back to my place, climbed the stairs and entered my apartment. I hit the light switch, tossed my hat and coat onto the couch, before walking to the bathroom and washing my hands and face. I put iodine on the cut on my forearm where the blade had cut through my sleeve.

From the dresser I got a tumbler and half-full bottle of scotch, opened the window to let in the evening air and the incessant sounds of the city. I sat on the foot of the bed, drank scotch and smoked cigarettes.

"The plot thickens," I finally muttered aloud.

I killed the scotch, stripped naked and got into bed. I slept.

Chapter Fourteen

The remnants of last night's storm were still on display Wednesday morning, August 7th. The brooding overcast sky matched my mood, a result of my brutal encounter the night before. I sat chain smoking on the seventh floor of the county courthouse, awaiting my turn on the witness stand for a crappy divorce case I had worked the previous month. I watched a flickering shaft of emerging sunlight paint a broken golden track across the polished floor of the sweltering hallway as I burned half-a-pack of smokes waiting for my turn on the stand.

Sometime in the second hour of me cooling my heels, the judge's clerk, Linda, appeared from chambers and told me I was free to go because the parties had settled. I scowled at her back as she returned to the courtroom.

There's a poor assumption people get from reading detective novels: that a private detective is always working on *the case*. Like he's got nothing else to do, and if someone hires him, he immediately drops everything and starts working just for them. In practice, I handled two to three wandering husband jobs a week along with the associated court appearances.

I picked up my Wilton and briskly walked down the stairs and out of the newly built marble courthouse. Standing at the top of the stone front steps outside, I snapped my Zippo, lit a fag and headed down the courthouse steps.

I noticed the flag on the pole in front of the courthouse hung languidly in the still air. Near its base, a few old rounders were lounging, chewing Bull Durham and spitting at the pigeons on the lawn. I stopped and watched one particular old nut open a bag of crumbs and feed the pigeons. When a couple of them hopped up on his hands, he glanced at me proudly.

The remaining old timers looked as if they'd been waiting a long time for something lucky or interesting to happen to them, a jury verdict or a police siren or an offer for a free drink.

The last man standing in this line of legal experts wore a tattered brown fedora pulled down over a receding hairline. His well-worn pinstripe suit was held up with narrow red suspenders. He wore dark sunglasses that covered his once famous dark browns that now resided over dark sunken cheek bones. Stepping off the last marble step of the purported building of justice, I caught the lawyer buttoning his suit coat, smile at me and put his hand out.

"Hey, mister, could you please help a blind man and spare a buck so I could have my first square meal in a week?"

I tilted my hat back and smirked. "You mean your first shot of the day, Terry?"

"Hey, Lou!" he said with a little more animation.

"How are you doing, Terry?" I asked as I headed down the pavement toward the strange little group.

"Sorry I didn't recognize you, Lou. Must be these dark cheaters," he said vaguely.

Grinning, I asked, "How's business, Terry?" I was genuinely interested. Terry McMalley had been a hell of a criminal lawyer for years. He had even thrown me work from time to time. But ever since his fiery Irish wife had run off with some fast talking New York producer who'd promised her she could dance on Broadway, he had become a gentleman lush.

Terry set down his well-worn, empty brown legal case and stuck his hands in his pockets. "I've had it better."

I smiled and slid him a sawbuck tucked inside my palm as we shook hands. He pocketed the fin quickly.

"Put it all on a number and you can retire, maybe," I said with a joking smile. "What do you like for today?"

"I usually stick with my house number, 215."

"All right, play a buck for me."

"I'll get it in. Where's the money?"

"Take it out of the five. Wasn't for me you wouldn't have anything to bet."

Saying goodbye, I walked to the corner towards the Hightower building. Some white-haired bag stood there on the pavement, rattling a red tin can. Pushing it up into my face, she gave me a pitch-smile as she asked, "Please help fight polio?"

"Let the government shell out the dough for it. They're always spending money like water," I stated.

"We must all chip in and do our part," she said sweetly. She probably worked for a percentage of the take.

"Your sexy smile does it, sister," I said, dropping a couple of dimes in the tin can.

"Thank you, would you like to put this on your coat?" She held up a red tin button shaped like a sword.

"They giving medals for being a sucker now?" I asked, winking at her and walking on.

Crossing Hudson, I came to the front door of my office building. Deciding I was too hungry to get anything done upstairs, I pressed past the entryway, jaywalked across the street and jumped into my awaiting coupe, started up the big-six and pointed the front bumper north.

I required a grilled ham-and-cheese sandwich, and the best hot version in town could only be found at Sieber's Coffee Shop, located on the first floor of the Sieber Hotel. The shop was one of those joints where they slice roast beef as thin as paper and specialized in vegetable plates for the woman as they wait for their slot in the beauty parlor.

Twenty minutes later, I strolled into the café just in time for the noonday rush. Being August, the place was crowded with women in brightly colored cotton summer dresses with their kids in shorts displaying sunburned knees.

From my table by the window, I watched the bevy of young women coming and going from the beauty parlor next door. Both the coffee shop and beauty parlor were fixtures of the Sieber Hotel complex. It was a bright and warm day, so I sat enjoying my grilled ham and cheese sandwich along with a cold glass of milk while I viewed the local talent.

Drinking some milk, I thought to *myself no matter how smart you think you are, you have to have a place to start from, such as a name, an address, or a point of reference.* All I had was an unsigned letter and a couple of names of people in Deep Deuce. I decided to make something of the day and believed the best place to start was seeing the people Lauren had mentioned from the Deuce music scene.

Finishing lunch, I laid two dollars down on the counter for the sandwich and the tip, walked out to the Ford, revved the engine before making a U-turn, and gliding south on Hudson towards the Deuce.

Driving over, I worked out some innocent-sounding questions to get one of the locals talking. Proceeding along Hudson, I passed the Calvary Baptist Church and turned down the hill to the heart of the Deuce.

The engine rattled to a stop as I reached into the glove compartment, pulled out a police sap and slid under my belt beneath my jacket. The sap was just in case my intrusion into the jazz community wasn't well received.

I headed toward the Littlepage Hotel where Mrs. Camp had said Thomas worked as the desk clerk, hoping he may have some ideas on who may be bothering her. I strode the pavement till I noticed the blue neon sign of the hotel declaring *No Vacancy*. I continued past the entrance to the corner and checked out the sides and back of the building. No fire escape or rear doors. I turned and walked back to the front door.

When I put my hand on the door, I noticed in the window a large green placard printed in blocked black letters advertising that Cab Calloway, the Hi-de-ho king of jazz and his orchestra were playing Wednesday and Thursday night at the Aldridge Theatre. When I finished reading, I assumed a self-important look and stepped into the hotel lobby.

There was a cool stillness in the lobby as I observed a trim colored man sitting behind the counter in a spotless white shirt and a rusty red tie. His black hair was slicked and marcelled in the fashion of the local musicians. He remained seated with a "no-comment" expression on his face. I knew getting information out of this or any hotel clerk in the Deuce was like opening a can of sardines without a key.

"Busy?" I asked him.

"Nope," he replied as he laid yesterday's copy of the *Black Dispatch* onto the desk, leaving it open to the article *"Fugitive Lady Scores" as romantic triumph at the Jewel Theater.*

He wasn't the type that if you asked for the time, he told you how the clocked worked. So I decided on a different approach, "I've got a car outside that needs a tire changed. About five bucks' worth of work. Know anyone that can help me out?"

The clerk didn't bite. He wasn't the type. His face became more businesslike. "Sounds like a lot of work on a hot August day. It might take more than five bucks to get such a job completed before sunset. Besides, you look stuffy to me and stuffy people bore me. What else you want, brother?" He scowled.

"I hear this is the homestead for most of the Blue Devils when they're playing in town."

He gave a relaxed smile as he tried to pitch me out of the field of play. "I keep hoping we'll get a storm soon," he said with a sigh. "We could use the rain, you know, something to break this heat wave we've been having. The clouds keep forming in the southwest every afternoon, but nothing happens."

Pulling my jacket off and swinging it over my shoulder, I pushed on him harder. "So do those musicians cause you any trouble when they hole up here?"

He stood more erect and asked, "What would that be to you, brother?"

"Nothing in particular, just I'm an old acquaintance of a skin tickler by the name of Sticks Timons. Thought I would drop in and say hello."

The desk man replied slowly, "He ain't around." And then with a growl asked, "What you really want, ofay?"

"Not much. But do you happen to know when Thomas comes back on today? Maybe he could use a few extra bucks."

He smiled the faintest smile I had seen in a while. "Five bucks is nice money for a working man, but it falls a little short and don't buy you that kind of information down here, mister. I suggest you save your fin and go have lunch at the Huffman's Lunch Room. Besides, it's my job if I get any kickback helping you."

I stepped to the desk. "You won't. I've got important people behind me.

91

So maybe I should talk to Junius or Louise; they own this joint, right? And I'm a private dick down here trying to help one of their friends," I fudged.

He looked confused, so I ask him directly. "Would Hamilton buy me anything?" I put a ten note under the night bell.

He quickly pulled the note and slipped it into his pocket. "Brother, you're still a little short. Maybe you should come back at six o'clock and ask Thomas if he can change your tire."

Smiling, I told him, "Thanks anyway," and exited back onto the street. The searing sun had almost reached its zenith, turning my cotton dress shirt damp and beads of perspiration to form on my face as I walked down the street. There was barely enough breeze to cool one side of my face. It was too hot to make a living outside, so with lessening caution, I cut diagonally across the intersection towards the Aldridge Theatre, hoping it was cooler and more productive inside.

The round ornate pillar clock in front of Robinson's Drugstore on Second Street showed just shy of two o'clock when I pulled the chrome framed glass door to the theater and went in. I noticed the place was as dark as midnight except for the eerie glow of the dozen or so Art Deco wall sconces and the red exit light over my head. Near the rear of the auditorium, I saw a lone lightbulb glowing over a large wooden coming from the manager's office. Next to where I stood, I noticed a tiny cubbyhole of an office with a small desk light on.

The shimmer of the light went out as the figure of a large man stepped into the door frame. He set down his half-empty canned beer of Krueger's Cream Ale on a barstool and proceeded to walk toward me. He didn't move his arms as he walked, but his footsteps were soft as ashes. When he came into the dim light coming from exited sign above my head, I observed that his general manner gave him the appearance of a rather rough-looking customer, and a fairly exotic specimen in his perfectly cut, white dress shirt.

His sleeves were rolled up to his elbows, exposing forearms as thick as the head of a Louisville Slugger. His head gave the illusion of a large black bowling ball sitting atop a huge white icebox. His rather large nose had a hump in it—evidently broken at some point. He stood at least six-six. His sheer size was his most notable feature. When he stopped in front of me, I felt like I had just stepped onto the Green Bay Packers' sideline rather than into a jazz joint. The man was definitely in good shape. With a voice that started deep in his huge chest, but echoed through the place like a low whisper, "Something I can do for you, mister?"

Reaching into my suit pocket, I pulled out a pack of cigarettes and my chrome lighter. Looking over the flame of the Zippo as I touched it to the fag, I took a drag while tucking my shirt in with my other hand, stopping at the pear-shaped sap tucked into my pants. I quickly decided that even if I had to use it, it wouldn't put a dent into this icebox. So I let it remain hidden, for the time being, anyway.

"Maybe. I'm guessing your name is George, then?"

A scowl deepened across his face. "You guess? You happen to see any other guys in the room?"

"No, I assume you're him. Even if you won't say you're him."

He nodded and remained still, watching me. He apparently had a vocabulary only slightly larger than a grade schooler. I reached into my inside jacket pocket, removed my wallet, flipped it open and flashed him my PI buzzer. He snatched it out of my hand and held it in the glow of the red exit sign.

He ran his sausage size fingers over his bald head as he stared down at my buzzer. "That don't carry any weight down here, mister. You'll have to do better than that." He stated handing my wallet back.

Digging into my front pocket, I pulled out a brass money clip, removed a fin and slowly placed it inside his shirt pocket. "I was hoping you might point me in the right direction on a case I'm looking into."

He appeared to be satisfied. "What kind of case, cowboy?"

"Protecting a very beautiful innocent," I replied.

"We is all innocent in the Deuce, you know that, right?" he replied as he backed up a step, giving me a conspiratorial smile. "And, of course, I don't know anything about anything. Like they say, poor old George is the last to know what's what. So why don't you turn around and snoop elsewhere."

Improvising, I said, "Mrs. Camp said you would help me out."

He looked at the polished tile floor between his feet. I could hear an electric clock somewhere in the silent office behind him, whirring like the thoughts in George's head. Finally he said, "You a friend of Miss Camp?"

I nodded in the affirmative.

He walked like a crippled ex-ballplayer into his compact private office. I followed and saw him open a desk drawer. A heavy automatic appeared in his hand, but he didn't point it at me. He pushed it down inside the front of his trousers and tucked in the back of his shirt while he staring at me there in the doorway. "You don't look like the kind of dude that has the salad it takes to travel in her circle, brother."

I nodded. "But, surprising as that might seem, it's still true."

The self-declared defender of Lauren stepped forward and smiled with jovial lechery. Clearly the image of the beautiful blonde had filled his mind as he spoke aloud to no one in particular. "That woman makes me need to walk around in the rain."

I let the comment slide. It didn't take a Valentino to know this woman inspired admirers everywhere she ventured. "I think she has that effect on all of us." I smiled in a twisted sideways grin and asked as I tried to push by him into the club. "Is the manager around?"

He put out his hand, stopping me in mid-stride, and held me there. He appeared to double in size as he declared, "Miss Cecelia's in the office, but she too busy to mess with you. So you'll have to deal with me."

"Maybe I should speak to Miss Zelia then?" Jackson had told me at one time that Zelia N. Page Breaux managed the theater, so I gave it a shot.

He shook his elephantine head as he edged closer and gripped my arm. "Miss Breaux ain't here. It's just Miss Cecelia and me and, and like I said, Miss Cecelia's too busy for whatever you're selling."

Slipping his grip, I placed another Lincoln in his shirt pocket. He paused as he forced the limited number of gears in his head to function and give a safe answer. "I suppose Miss Cecelia could spare a few minutes."

The telephone on his desk chirred. He picked up the receiver and gruffly barked. "Oh sorry, I've been busy, keeping the riffraff out before the club opens...yes, I'll be home after work...of course, I'm alright. Yes, I'll see you when I get home." He hung up, shrugged, and in direct contradiction to his earlier stance said, "Go on back."

Turning and rambling toward the back office, I noticed a long string of black-and-white autographed pictures lining the wall of the club. I slowed my pace and looked more closely. Some I was familiar with, while some others I had to try to read their scrawls on the Kodak to get a clue. The first I knew, Miss Zelia, followed by Cab Calloway, the King of Scat, and the local greats, Charles Christian and Jimmy Rush. Next I recognized a photo of the Blue Devils followed by one of Count Basie. The final snapshot was of a curvaceous, beautiful ebony woman dressed in a white tuxedo with tails and a top-hat. I didn't recognize her, so I stopped and looked at her bold autograph more closely.

Direct from the Clam House in New York City, Gladys Bentley.

I stood straight and grinned to myself *I bet that's a show worth seeing.* Still smiling, I walked on towards the back office where an attractive woman in her late twenties wearing dungarees and a pale, cream-colored cotton top leaned on the door frame awaiting my approach.

She was like a wildflower from an old-fashioned garden. Her soft, luxurious hair was shingled into a thousand short, black curls that kept running into one another, accenting her tiny, freckled brown nose. She was tall and well-proportioned, with flecked greenish brown eyes that took on a copper glint when the ceiling light hit them just right. She had a mouth that was a bit heavy and quite wide, but devoid of lipstick. The lips maintained a whisk of a smile that never left her face, labeling her a gentle person. I couldn't get over it. Her fingers played nervously on a string of bracelets worn around her left wrist. The bracelets caught my attention. There were eight of them, Chinese, of intricate design, amber, gold, carved ivory, and jade. They made a particular clanking sound whenever she moved her arm. I could not help myself from admiring Miss Cecelia May.

Most men would suggest that there are hundreds of women in the world as resplendent as Cecelia. But the expressions these women wear for the outside world betrays them. Their faces show arrogance or petulance, but that's all right because their desirability and sexuality make up for it. You know they will be coy and demur for a short time. But once you've become accustomed to their beauty, only their arrogance or petulance remain.

Cecelia wore her own face for the world to see. It projected the expressions of strength and humility and decentness. Should you become accustomed to Cecelia's raw attraction, there still would be strength and decentness. This was a girl a man could hurt. She was the type of woman that required a man's loyalty and deserved it.

"I guess I'm staring," I said sheepishly.

"I'm used to it in this place, but some I appreciate more than others," she said sweetly as she whirled and headed back to the chair behind the desk that sat below the eight-paned window in the rear.

I stepped into her office that was decorated with a woven green rug that lay beneath varnished wood desk with a stack of manila folders strewn over the top. The top drawer of one of three filing cabinets had been pulled clear out so its load of manila folders had spilled on the floor. I gave the once-over to the large steel safe behind the desk and registered the fact that the cabinets and the safe could be viewed through the window where any passing policeman could make sure they hadn't been tampered with.

After Cecelia slipped into the large leather office chair behind her desk, she pointed to the chairs in front and told me to take a seat.

I eased myself into the closest chair with my story ready, one that was nearly the unadorned truth or as close to it as the situation would allow. I'm a great one for the obvious, because it saves a lot of fiddling around. But I figured I should start with a polite question, first.

"Can I ask what you do here?"

"Everything." She grinned while shaking her head. "No, not really, but I do manage this place for Miss Zelia, so she can carry on with her teaching duties."

"She pays you well?" I inquired.

"I get a good salary and she gives me a percentage off the top as well, and she also lets me sing on Tuesday nights when we're slow."

"Sounds like a good gig."

She smiled, looking pert, and said, "I'm sure you're not down here to interview for a new job, so how can I help you?"

Deciding it was best to discard any tricky stuff with this skirt, I came out cold-turkey. "My name's Lou Nayland and I'm working a case that involves a woman who may have gotten herself mixed up in a jam with some locals who frequent the clubs along Second Street."

I showed her my buzzer and removed a newspaper clipping with a photo of Mrs. Camp from my suit vest pocket and handed it to Cecelia. "You know her?" I said in a reasonable tone.

Cecelia looked at it and made a sound that might have been a laugh. If it was, it was the un-merriest laugh I'd ever heard in my life. "Yeah, I've seen that dumb-Dora in here. She looks like what she is, a jezebel rolling her eyes and shaking her goodies at all the young musicians here in the Deuce. She's nothing but trouble," she concluded coldly.

I nodded almost imperceptibly. "Are you saying she's been stirring up trouble for you recently?"

"Far as I can tell, that bird stirs up trouble anywhere she goes," she said with passion.

I nodded back with a look of interest. "Has she caused you a specific piece of difficulty lately?"

"No, I couldn't say that, she's just trouble in general," she stated vigorously.

"So it's more of an indeterminate nature, then?" I said, trying not to look too interested, but my ears were cocked for every word.

"Let's just say I prefer she go somewhere else to entertain her ass."

"Fair enough, but since she isn't and hasn't, what's she done that makes her persona non grata with you."

She made her eyes small. "For one, she's a married broad. For another, she's bad for business. She makes my usual crowd nervous."

"In what way does she make your regulars feel nervous?" I asked.

"Mostly it's how she rolls in here acting high and mighty," she stated coldly.

"That's it?" I said.

"Mostly, but it gets worse when some local girl catches her spreading the butter with the colored band members," she said in a bitter tone.

"She cornered anyone in particular?" I asked.

"Mostly Sticks Timons, you know, the skin tickler for the Blue Devils."

I nodded and asked, "Do you know this Timons guy well?"

"Yeah, you could say I know him pretty well," she acknowledged. "But I know most of the musicians that play here in the Deuce as well as most of our regulars."

"How well do you know this, Timons?" I asked.

"To be honest with you, Mr. Nayland, we were a couple once, but not anymore," she said steadily.

"Care to tell me about it?"

"Everyone around here knows the story, so I'll tell ya. Our relationship started five years ago. Somehow it seems longer than five. Anyway, I worked at Ruby's Grill as a waitress when he first came in from Kansas City looking to move onto the local scene," she said crisply. "At first he dated a friend of mine, Judy Warren. It went on for a couple of weeks until they had a spat about the same time I'd broken off with a trumpet player with another band. So when he asked me out, I went. And we went together from then on. Everybody thought we'd get married. I guess I did too. But then things changed. He seemed to lose interest in me as his music career took off and we drifted apart."

I had been prepared for a string of lies. But I knew she was being straight with me, and I suspected that she was telling more of it than she had intended. Every syllable was a personal pain for her even to speak. So I asked a directed question. "Were you in love with him?"

Cecelia's voice broke as the sadness seeped in. "I thought I was. Otherwise we wouldn't have been so close. But maybe it wasn't love. See, we were both part of the in crowd and we both liked to dance. Everyone we knew just expected us to go together. It seemed right to other people, so their desires became ours. Maybe we just fell in love with the idea of being in love with one another." She looked at me through a fog of doubt. "Do you understand?"

I nodded. "Of course."

"When it finally ended, it hurt badly. At least for me it did. Because I had come to realize, deep down, he was the love of my life. But he moved on."

She sighed as her mouth moved over her words as if they were giving her bitter nourishment. "To be honest, he's always been more into his music career than any particular dame. Guess that would have been alright if we had gotten married, at least on my part it would have." She lowered her eyes, not so much in shame as in a submission to the facts.

I waited patiently before I proceeded with a more general inquiry. "May I ask, apart from your personal history, what kind of man he is?"

"He's a dedicated musician, popular with the crowds, and I still believe he's a good and decent man." She smiled without looking happy. "He's too damn nice for that ofay dame, that's for damn sure."

I just nodded and sat in silence, hoping her talkativeness hadn't ended.

"She'll bring nothing but ruin to his life," she uttered with a touch of fearfulness.

Then I saw the eyes cool. "But the poor sap is dizzy for her. Can't help himself, people say. But I know she'll destroy him or his career before she's through with him, damn ofay. She was born with wickedness in her blood," she said with a touch of hatred.

The expression on her face brought me a twinge of sorrow, but I agreed without saying it aloud. I, too, believed it was going to end badly for Timons and Lauren or both.

After she composed herself, I thought it safe to intrude further. "Do you know anyone who might have it in for them?"

Her eyes were evasive. "No one."

"Would it surprise you to know that the pair does more than dance and cuddle in your club?"

Cecelia's face developed a red tinge to it. "So it is true, then? I'd hoped it was just tittle-tattle. I wasn't certain, but I suspected it. Because it made me sick to think that it could be going on. That woman is total trash."

"Would you have any idea who has anything to gain by exposing them?"

There were about ten seconds of quiet before she spoke. "No, not really, and to be frank, most of the people down here know. So revealing it wouldn't cause anyone waves in this neighborhood," she said stonily. "If there is a threat, it would only concern the twist, not Timons."

She stood up. "Mr. Nayland, I believe your answer lies in mid-town or up-town, but not down here. Thank you for listening to my story. I hope you can help your client, especially if it helps that bitch never return to my club again. But now I've got to make arrangements for Jimmy Rushing's farewell performance here at the club Friday night before he joins Count Basie's in New York."

I stood up and stuck out my hand. Without looking, she shook it and began to read the account books that covered her desk. I turned, left the office and walked back toward the exit where I stuck my head into the small dog box, where George sat reading the *Black Dispatch*. I thanked him and left.

I arrived back at my office door by mid-afternoon. The reception room was still empty except for the mail which had scattered across the floor. I gathered it up, walked through the door marked "PRIVATE" and tossed the sorted envelopes onto my desk just as the phone rang. I picked it up on the third ring. "Hello."

"Afternoon, Mr. Nayland. I hope I'm not disturbing you."

"No," I replied, "just desk clearing. How can I help you?"

"Well, I'm checking to see if you might be available to come by my grandmother's house for lunch tomorrow? Father won't be present, but it will give you an opportunity to meet and question the rest of my family."

"I think I can make that. What time and where?" I asked.

"Good, say around 11:30. The address is 216 NW 16th Street. I've told grandmamma that I'm inviting a friend of Johnny's who's in town working and squared you an invite," she said. "See you then." She hung up.

Chapter Fifteen

The house sat in the upscale neighborhood of the Heritage Hills district of the city. It wasn't the largest structure on 16th Street, but it was still a damn big, solid red brick house highlighted with stone trimmed windows. The front was dominated by four stone columns built across the forefront. It was made to appear even larger from the street due to the red terra-cotta slate roof whose wide overhang gave the house an appearance of being enormous for its squat two stories.

Bringing my car to a stop at the curb, I noticed a small Asian man in a straw hat of indeterminate age kneeling shoulder-deep among the roses with a pair of clippers in his gloved hand. I strolled up the pavement as the man rose to his feet and watched me approach porch. He then stepped carefully among the bushes to the next bush, still keeping his eyes on me as I continued up onto the expansive porch that lay behind the beautifully manicured green front lawn. I actually reflected that the gardener must be damn good and had performed quite a feat to maintain such luscious growth in the month of August in Oklahoma. When I had reached the two Doberman Pincher stone statues that guarded the manor house, I complimented him.

"You maintain a beautiful lawn," I stated. "Most lawns in this season have all since turned brown."

He nodded his appreciation and said thanks in heavily accented tone. A hint of cruelty curled on his lips as he smiled back lazily in my direction. I wondered briefly if he might be the one behind the extortion letters, but quickly concluded that a man of his social position would most likely want money exchange for his silence rather than demanding a change in Lauren's behavior. The gardener continued to grin quizzically at me while I was chased these thoughts around my dull mind standing there admiring the greenery. I grinned back at him. That being the only response you can give an elderly Asian.

He continued the trimming of the verge as I noticed Lauren's blue Packard as well as a two-door blue Nash Breezer parked in the drive. I stared down both the stone Dobermans as I mounted the steps in one stride. The front door had an oversized brass knocker that said my tie was crooked. I straightened it and rang the bell.

With nothing happening and no one appearing, I pushed the bell again and reflected on all I knew about the Davis family that resided inside this storybook setting. There were the questionable oil leases dealings and deaths connected to the family's drilling business, the financial rewards of which had granted the family social standing and a degree of influence on local and state politics. Then there were the deaths of Lauren's parents, nothing unusual there, and there was the fight between the siblings ten years back. Frankly, none of which seemed very helpful to my investigation.

No one appeared, so I knocked on the door. After which I heard the slow shuffling sounds of feet as a middle-aged sour puss in a butler's uniform opened the door six inches, the exact extent the chain on the door allowed. He gave me his best fake upper-class stare and asked with a degree of bitter lemons in his voice. "May I help you?"

"Lou Nayland," I said. "I'm a calling on Johnny and Lauren Camp. I believe I'm expected for lunch?"

He let me come in as the heavy front door creaked closed behind me. The fake British butler left me standing on the front landing and stated in his terrible accent, "Let me announce your arrival. Please wait here."

I advanced a few steps and placed my hat on the oriental stool as I took a survey of the place. I was in a large square foyer, as high and dim as a hayloft. A large staircase stretched up to the private quarters above. There were expensive etched glass French doors on the right, I cupped my hands over the pane of glass and peered inside. I could vaguely make out the outline of a large formal dining table with accommodations for twelve. A large sterling bowl filled with an array of summer flowers served as the table's centerpiece. The cost of the bowl alone would have allowed me time-off for three years.

Though nobody was in sight, I heard voices coming from the rear of the house. So I peeked into the French doors opposite the dining room. The room was a large living room, so large in fact you could play catch in. The newly introduced game of Monopoly sat on a coffee table. The remainder of the furniture was a mish-mash of last century, Art Deco and southwest, so was all the bric-à-brac the family had scattered onto and into every table top, wall and niche. All of which was of the type that only the rich can make seem eloquent. The only redeeming feature in the room was a large modern painting hung over the stone fireplace. A small dog of mixed breeding sat in a colorful Queen Anne chair next to the fireplace. She seemed to be the master of the room, like some queen of old. I suspected she reflected the personality of her owner in many respects.

Becoming bored staring down the dog, I looked for a place to wait with more dignity. Discovering nothing to sit on other than the stool I had laid my hat. I believed this now to be intentional, being no point in making unwanted arrivals feel at home.

So I went over and sat on the third step of the staircase just as the French doors to the living room suddenly opened and Lauren emerged donning a floral pink day dress. She glided over to me, gave me a socially acceptable hug for a friend of her husband and quickly stepped back and with a sweeping gesture stated, "Won't you join us in the sun room and I'll introduce you to the family." She stepped aside and proclaimed, "This way."

We preceded though the living room towards the rear of the house. As we did so I noticed a large sterling silver picture frame atop the mantel over the fireplace. The picture displayed two young people, a boy and a girl, each about nine or ten along with a pair of beautiful blonde, young adults. I figured this was Lauren's family before her parents had passed. We continued through across an expensive Persian rug.

We continued through another set of French doors into a brightly sunlit flagstone porch filled with an array of semi-tropical plants and orchids growing up from terra-cotta pots. A small breeze drifted in through the open windows.

A distinguished older woman with a cameo pin at her throat, who I assumed was Lauren's grandmother, sat in a large wicker chair, deep and comfortable. The old gal immediately gave me two surprises. At first glance, her eyes appeared to be small and undistinguished. But when she looked up at me, I noticed they were quite large, somber, very dark and certainly shrewd. She was remarkably youthful looking, though she had pewter colored hair, slicked back and tied into a bun. The old gal wore a long necklace composed of a double strand of perfectly white pearls which were accompanied by two hazel nut size pearl earrings. Her long legs tucked under the chair were not painful to look at as well, and I decided she must have been a bearcat in her day as Lauren introduced me.

"Mr. Nayland, this is my grandmother Della Mae. Mother, this is Lou Nayland, a good friend of Johnny's who's in town to scout a baseball game this weekend."

When Lauren finished, her grandmother stood and extended a hand. I instantly noticed she still maintained a long and lanky figure within her sleek black dress. Lauren had come from good stock.

"Afternoon, Mrs. Davis, nice to meet you." I still possessed sufficient manners when my job required, so I took her outstretched hand. It was strong and firm.

Della Mae introduced her elderly female companion sitting in the adjacent wicker chair. "This is my dear friend, Mandy Slick."

Her manner was impersonal, but gracious as she turned and introduced a relatively handsome young man with thin lips that formed downward slightly. His pale blue eyes were set beneath eyebrows that were trimmed too thin, giving him a look of a blonde hair milquetoast.

"This is my grandson, Brock," she said. The boy nodded in my direction with slight disdain and remained seated in the corner of the wicker couch.

He looked back down at a richly bound lettered book. The gold lettering on the binding read *Titus Andronicus*. He had a light blue tennis shirt with a blue silk scarf tied about his neck. I've always had an idea, probably incorrectly, that I could handle any man who wore a silk ascot. The shirt contrasted well with his white tennis slacks that narrowed atop a pair of lightly colored oxford shoes, the soles of which were made of red rubber.

His grandmother cleared her throat. The wrinkle between his eyebrows deepened as he glared back at her and pushed himself off the couch. When he stood he was still shorter than me by two inches. He shook my hand. His grip was not nearly as firm as his grandmother's.

"Nice to meet you, Mr....?" He stated in a low-ended tenor voice. I noted that grammatical solecisms had been weeded out of his speech, but nothing had been put in their place. His voice was impersonal and lifeless.

"Lou Nayland," I replied politely.

Lauren's brother didn't impress me. He reminded me of the typical cloistered type that hadn't done an honest day's work his entire life. He clearly had been pampered and shielded from the real world by an overly protective family, and it showed in his soft hands.

Turning to his grandmother and the other guest, he announced, "I'm sorry, Mother, but I can't stay for lunch. I must finish my lecture on the plays I'm presenting to my students in English Literature class on Monday. I also have plans to attend Miss Sister Aimee Semple McPherson's Revival meeting tonight down on the Canadian River."

He walked around Lauren without acknowledging she was even alive and kissed his grandmother on the cheek. He walked through the French doors and called back, "Pleased to have met you, Mr. Nayland."

I turned back to the ladies. The look on Lauren's face would have wilted lesser men, but her stare was directed toward her brother and not me.

Lauren's grandmother watched Brock exit the room as she spoke to me with a dark smirk. "He's known as a blatant snob and notorious jellybean in our social circle." With a sweeping gesture, she led the group into the dining room.

After we had all been seated in the formal dining room, the butler reappeared. Mrs. Davis ordered Old Fashioneds for the entire lunch party. When he departed, she looked at all of those gathered and quickly detailed her story and the recipe.

"I'm sorry the drinks will only be passable, because it takes a good woman to make a first class Old Fashioned." Sitting straighter in her chair she continued, "You have to muddle the sugar, water and bitters properly, you know, and then you toss in the ice and good whiskey and then carefully twist a lemon peel on top. Like anything else, it's simply a matter of following the recipe." The butler reappeared with our drinks as the cook placed a creamy soup before us.

When we were just four again, Mrs. Davis continued in her polite way, "You must forgive my grandson, Mr. Nayland. He's what they call a bookworm. Always has been. I heard it said he's a genius, or pretty close to it, but I swear he needs somebody to tell him to come in out of the rain. But now he's a professor, you know, at the university and teaches literature in the English Department. I hope he can find a girlfriend and begin his life. But such ordinary things don't seem to hold his attention much. He believes himself destined in some way to change the world. He's totally obsessed with English authors and that McPherson woman." She smiled again. I liked her smile.

She gave me a short family history of how Mr. Lawrence had the good fortune to find large deposits of oil in Northern Oklahoma and how it enabled the family to give generously to St. Luke's and other deserving charities in the community, about which she spoke with great pride. She extolled his recent accomplishment of pushing and funding the rebuilding of Douglas High School for the colored community.

She continued with the sad story of how Lauren's parents had succumbed to the Spanish Flu after the Great War, and it fell upon Mr. Davis and her to raise their young grandchildren. She spoke with gratification of how they both had gone to university and become such fine young Christian adults and how lucky Lauren was to marry the nice young man, Johnny. Though she knew nothing about baseball or what Johnny really did for a job, she spoke with admiration of him, a feeling I actually shared, though mine was based on his baseball skills rather than his character.

At the conclusion of lunch, Mrs. Davis ordered the butler to bring sangrias for our small party as she explained, "The drink is a mild concoction of sugar, orange juice and port wine."

When the drinks arrived, I politely drank the sweet liquor and smiled at each of the ladies, thinking to myself that I had to admit the old gal knew how to drink properly.

When we'd all finished our drinks, I pushed myself back from the table as I looked significantly at each of the women as I spoke. "Thank you all for the informative conversation and the lovely lunch, but now you must all excuse me. I have some interviews with a couple of baseball prospects at Holland Field before this afternoon's batting practice."

I gathered my hat and closed the front door behind me. The lunch had been pleasant but not fruitful in furtherance of my investigation. With the possible exception of the knowledge that Lauren's brother, Brock, was apparently seriously into Sister Aimee McPherson, but I wasn't sure yet how that small tidbit of information had any connection to Lauren's case.

I broke out in a sweat as I crossed the paving stones set firmly in the lawn, when suddenly Lauren stepped out onto the porch and asked, "May I have a few words with you before you leave?" I turned slowly, faced her and nodded. She quickly stepped down from the porch and met me in the grass as we ambled slowly in the direction of my parked car.

For a moment her eyes seemed to have something akin to panic in them. "I received another letter," she stated as she removed a manila envelope from under her arm and handed it to me. I took it from her, opened the flap and removed several five-by-seven, black-and-white photos. There were three photos in all; each displaying images of a tall elegant blonde and a handsome well-dressed colored man with his arm wrapped around her waist walking across a street. The photos were taken from the rear and didn't show either of the party's faces.

"Is this a recent picture of the two of you?" I asked.

She bit her lip. "I believe it was from two Fridays ago."

I turned a picture over and read a message written in large block letters.

Let marriage be honorable among all, and let the marriage bed be without defilement. Repent or evil doers shall be revealed and struck down!

I looked at her. "I can only assume these represent more verses from the bible?"

"Hebrews again," she answered sharply.

"It's not much of a clue to go on, but I've some possible new avenues to explore. Maybe they'll shed some light on who is behind this. Please call if you receive anything else or are contacted in any way." She was near sobbing as I finished.

She quickly smoothed her face and tried to look assured and went on looking like exactly what she was: a hard blonde beauty in her fading twenties, fighting the world with two weapons, sex and money. Her weapons were beginning to turn in her hands, creating emotional scars. "Mr. Nayland, you must make this end! I feel things coming to a head in this matter and I'm worried for Johnny. He's having a great summer and this could end it quickly if it becomes known. If it requires money, I'll find it. Just let me know."

I spoke in an even, professional tone in response. "You can see the great difficulty. So far it's a failure to find any indication of a motive, and like I said, it seems almost personal and therefore I doubt money is the solution. Motive's the key, and so far it's hidden from us, but I'll do everything to discern it as well as protect you and Johnny." She raised her eyes and managed a grateful smile.

I heard a door bang in the distance as I crossed the remainder of the yard. I noticed a sprinkler across the street had caught a rainbow in its net of spray. Above the treetops lining the street, the tower of the oil derrick that sat on Lincoln stood darkly against the sky, symbols both of law and order and prosperity. I looked back at the huge house. The small man with the clippers was standing at the corner of the house staring at me as I waved in his direction, but received no response. I kicked the starter savagely on the Ford as I noticed out of the corner of my eye that the Nash was no longer parked in the driveway. Deciding that it had belonged to the departed Brock I adjusted the rear-view mirror and pulled away from the curb.

Chapter Sixteen

The hot, stale air took away my good mood as I steered the coupe down the quiet residential street and turned south. I noticed a black funeral hearse that had been parked at the end of the block. Looking into my rear-view mirror, I caught a glimpse of the driver. He appeared to be a colored man with a blue fedora pulled down over a pair of sunglasses. I shrugged, thinking nothing of it, because most of the funeral homes in town used colored drivers in their processions.

As I drove toward my office, I observed the black hearse still following me several car lengths behind. I shrugged it off. But out of fun, I took the next left, passed by the Hughes Hotel Marion and turned right onto Broadway. Speeding the little coupe up as I drove quickly past the *Daily Oklahoman* building, glancing again in my side mirror as I clipped by the Playmore Bowling alley. I made out the large black oil burner was still tailing me. Passing the Skirvan Hotel, I veered in front of Old Dan pulling his Meadow Gold Milk Wagon, nearly kissing the curb as I took a quick right onto Grand and pushed the accelerator down, giving me some distance in case my stalker made the turn timely.

Looking into the mirror again, it become certain I had a tail. In a further attempt to shake him, I shot past the Biltmore Hotel and made a swift turn onto Harvey, sped north for several blocks and circled back onto Tenth. The black sedan was gone. So I let off the pedal, applied some brake, and sped past Perrine's Funeral Home. I became unnerved when I saw the hearse rolling down the street in my direction in my rear-view mirror. Waiting at the stop sign, I hoped the hearse would pull into Perrine's and that my

109

imagination was just getting the best of me. I removed my foot from the brake and made a hard right heading south, still keeping an eye in my rear-view mirror, anticipating the reappearance of the persistent dead man's touring car. The huntsman made the turn and was still following me four car-lengths behind. At the next open parking space, on the opposite side of the street, I made a quick U-turn and pulled into the vacant parking spot. The long sleek hearse with the man in a blue fedora hat sailed by me as I watched.

I sat for five minutes to see if the rolling meat-wagon would return. When it didn't, I pulled out and zigzagged through the side streets towards my office, never spotting the hearse again.

Before I entered my building, I took a few minutes to re-tie my shoelaces, checking up and down Hudson. The hearse never appeared. So I entered, walked to the brass elevator, pushed the up arrow, and said hello to the new girl working the elevator. We both remained silent as we rode the lift to the 5th floor.

The operator with tired, half-closed eyes told me to have a good evening as I stepped out into the freshly scrubbed hallway and proceeded to the door of my office. My reception room was empty of everything that could pay the rent except the smell of cigarette smoke and dust.

I stepped into the hot stickiness of my office and flipped on the ceiling fan, throwing my hat on the desk. I noted that I wasn't in the habit of giving my hats the respect that Jackson gave his Stetson.

Sitting in my steer-hided chair, I pulled my bottle of good scotch from the drawer. Using a filthy tumbler, I poured myself two fingers' worth.

The warming liquor burned its way down my pipe as I hoisted the city phone book onto the desk to confirm that Lauren and Johnny Camp resided at the Mayfair. I was playing with the idea of doing a reconnaissance job on the Camps' apartment to determine if they were being surveilled, but quickly discarded the idea as an unproductive use of my time.

Reaching for the scotch, I poured another drink just as the buzzer to the outer door went off. I heard heavy footsteps cross the tiled floor of the reception room and stop as the privacy door opened and a large colored man standing over six feet tall stepped forward and filled the opening.

I didn't like the looks of the man. His appearance was that of a gangster, and he reminded me of a hood named Henny who always wore beautiful, tailored slate-blue suits, exactly like this guy. Except the man before me now was colored, well-built, dressed to the Joe Brook's and definitely not a piker. He displayed a floral blue handkerchief stylishly tucked into his front breast pocket highlighting his matching tie, neither of which was cheap nor something Henny could of have pulled off.

He was a stout figure with a smooth, beautiful face and a straight jaw. He was cool, collected and without a sign of being bent. So I placed my .38 Police Positive back into in my top desk drawer and said, "Hire me or serve me." He missed my undeniable wit. "You here to give me the goof, or are you just slumming?"

"I'm here to do neither, Mr. Nayland, I've just come to chat." He grinned, his white teeth flashing in his dark face.

"Have a seat then, Mister...?"

"My name's Lesley Timons and I've come to speak with you regarding the tittle-tattle spreading in the Deuce that you're asking unpleasant questions that involve people I'm protective of. I'm speaking of course of those types of questions men of character don't talk about in public places."

"Before I answer your question, maybe you could answer a one for me. Were you tailing me today in a black hearse?"

"I was, my uncle lets me use it when I'm in town. Is that important?"

"No, I was just checking a fact," I replied.

He nodded and finished his thought. "I was following you, trying to discover who'd been you been talking to. However, after seeing you come out of the house on 16th and talk to a lady on the lawn, I reconsidered and thought it would better just to speak to in person, but you lost me before we good speak."

I remained as silent as an empty ballpark, so he continued. "But before we get into that any further, I'm curious to know if you are a friend or employee of the lady you were talking to."

I nodded in the affirmative.

Then he clearly stated, "If that's square, you should know, I'm not her enemy, either."

I nodded again before he asked, "Now that we've established we're both friends with the lady, what's your business with her?"

"I'm not sure how to answer that, Mr. Timons. You're going to have to be more specific, because I'm usually involved in a case that concerns a woman's or man's dirty laundry. And frankly, these people require me to complete my assigned tasks quietly and confidentially."

He grew larger as he spoke. "Then let me spell it out for ya then. You seem like a bright man, but a bright man can be too bright for his own good. You've got to learn to understand that you can't go around annoying people, especially important people like me. Further, what I do in my spare time and with who is none of your damn business no matter who's paying your rent," he barked.

I shook my head calmly. "Mr. Timons, I'm still not sure what we're talking about. But I will say that I believe our interests in this particular case are aligned. And if you must know, one of my current assignments is to prevent harm or public humiliation being laid before the door of a very nice lady that I believe we are both acquainted with."

He released his firm grip on the chair's armrests so I continued in the same even tone. "Now, if you care to help in that by giving me information that's advantageous to her case, I'll pour us both a drink and we can talk."

"It's possible I might," he said, clearing his throat heavily.

I reached down and pulled out another dirty tumbler and poured two fingers' worth and slid it over to Timons. He stopped talking as I poured. A woman would have chatted on, but a gentleman respects the ritual. After taking the glass, he swirled it several times, sniffed it slowly and then took a swig. Mr. Timons was a gentleman, I decided.

He looked back at me with an earnest plea. "Then, Mr. Nayland, could you be more reasonable and let me know what this is all about?"

I understood far too well what it took for a man of Timons' character to speak out loud he was seeking assistance in a personal matter and about something he cared about. But as much as I liked this guy sitting before me,

I had to protect my client's interests first.

So I played it cautiously. "Mr. Timons, I would like to give you a hypothetical situation. Say there's a young woman, a happily married woman, married to a local public figure. She enjoys the finer aspects of jazz music, and this woman's family is not currently aware of her fondness for jazz and its participants. Thirdly, let's surmise they would not approve of the young lady's taste in music, places where it's performed and those who perform it. Follow me so far?" I asked before taking a drink of my scotch.

He nodded yes as he also took another swig of my good scotch.

"Let's also say that the woman's husband knows of her taste in music and has no objections to enjoying the same. But here's the rub. Someone doesn't appreciate her hanging out and enjoying jazz music."

Timons nodded. "I follow so far, please continue."

I knew I was dancing on the edge of my cleats regarding PI-client privilege and it made my mouth dry, forcing me to take another taste of hooch.

When the scotch touched bottom, I continued with my hypothetical story. "Whoever it is that doesn't appreciate this particular lady's modern musical taste has now gone as far as to threaten her with exposure via a threatening letter."

He sat upright quickly, but spoke softly. "If that story was true I can see how the lady would be distressed. Would you care to tell me more surrounding your hypothetical story?"

I remained silent, so he continued. "If you did so, it's possible I could provide you with alterative solutions or avenues of inquiries. But to do so, I would need more details on what she told a particular private dick when securing his assistance in her matter." He took another sip and waited.

I tried not to appear put-out, but stated, "Don't ask me questions about what hypothetical woman said, because you know her statements are confidential."

His eyes darkened. "I see your point. But what if_?"

Before he finished his thought, I spoke. "Nor ones, concerning the investigation of said hypothetical story."

I knew there was no point in me cross-examining Timons because I might reveal details Lauren preferred to keep secret. I took a deep breath to take some wind out of my sails and attempted to conclude our discussion. "But I appreciate your offer to help this unknown hypothetical woman and I do believe you would aid me in her afflictions, Mr. Timons. I would need the hypothetical woman's permission to disclose a private conversation, even if it might aid her in her cause."

He sat in his chair quietly as the moments ticked by. Then abruptly he finished his drink in one swill, placed the glass on my desk, stuck out his hand to me and said, "Well then, no hard feelings, Mr. Nayland. I think we're both trying to protect the same muffin. I'll respect your protecting her for now, but if she does give you permission, please come see me first instead of wandering around the Deuce like a white rooster in a red hen chicken coop. It would better for everyone involved." He paused. "If there's anything you need, leave a message at the Littlepage with Thomas, the night clerk. He'll get it to me."

I acknowledged his request with a nod of my head as he quietly left.

When Lauren's lover left the office, I couldn't help but like the guy. He seemed to be carrying an aura of bad luck, like crossing a black cat or circling ravens overhead.

I looked at my watch, it was 2:30. I still had time to be productive. I decided I would head over and speak to the barber, David "Snips" Flatten. I figured it would be his slow part of his day.

Chapter Seventeen

The sporting news blared on the car's radio as I drove to Flattens barber shop.

> *Fifty thousand spectators packed Comiskey Park last night to see Joe Louis, the Detroit Brown Bomber, knock out King Levinsky, the Chicago Jewish fish-peddler, in 2 minutes and 21 seconds in the first round of a ten round bout. Levinsky sat on the tarp in his corner mumbling, "Don't let him hit me again, I'm through."*
>
> *Not since 1927, when Jack Dempsey and Gene Tunney fought before a record-breaking crowd in Soldier's Field...*

The radio announcer droned on as I pulled in front of Flattens Barber Shop on the corner of Walker and 12th. A bright full moon hung like a ghost in the sunlight. I thought of Irene as I peered inside the barber shop. The place seemed to be devoid of customers.

Flatten himself was a small bespectacled man with trim blond flat-topped hair and matching mustache with the stocky build of a wrestler. He had a pleasant bulldog face and sat in one of the three barber chairs, reading the sporting news. I pushed the door inward and entered with long strides. A bell overhead tinkled and then stopped as the door swung shut. I asked, "Are you free to give me a quick trim?"

He smiled, throwing the paper on the counter, and stood up. He escaped being a dwarf by a few inches. He pointed to the chair. "I think I might be able to squeeze you in. Have a seat."

I removed my coat, placed it and my hat upon the chrome racks by the door. I plopped down into the chair while observing the photos of different styles of cuts tacked to the spaces between the mirrors.

Flatten grabbed a cotton blue barber's gown and proceeded to pull it over my chest as he simultaneously snapped the top firmly around my neck with a small cotton sheet inside. I heard the little silver snaps click closed as he drew the collar firmly around my neck as I looked at his reflection in the mirror and noticed one ear resembled the head of cauliflower. He caught my inquisitive look as I pointed to my own ear and asked, "Have you done some boxing or wrestling?"

He replied eagerly, "I was a 126 pound wrestler for Oklahoma A & M's for two seasons in the 20s. Unfortunately, I wrestled behind Ross Flood, the three time national champ, so I didn't see much mat time in front of a crowd. But, during my third year, I tore my right knee out and had to come back home and pick up the barber trade." I nodded with respect.

"Just take a quarter off the sides and trim my neck," then finished my thought, "That's still a hell of an accomplishment." Truly meaning the compliment as Flatten nodded, but remained solemn.

"Anyway, my name's Lou Nayland and I'm a private detective working on a case."

"Nice to meet you, Mr. Nayland. I'm David Flatten, but my friends call me Snips," he stated as he continued to cut the black curls off the back.

"Sheriff Jackson gave me your name. Said if I was ever caught out in the rain, you would be the man to see. Well, it's raining hard, Mr. Flatten, and I could use some answers to some very hard questions. In particular, some difficult questions I have concerning members of a secret society that's well established in some parts around the state."

He continued his cutting with no indication he was in a talkative mood. So I continued, "Jackson suggested you might be able to help me out on a little private matter I'm working on, for a very nice lady."

The smile disappeared from his lips as he stopped cutting, placing his comb and scissors onto a towel spread out before the tubes of Barbicide. "Excuse me for a minute. I need to fill the spray bottle."

He walked to the back of the shop and closed the door behind him. Five minutes later he reappeared in the doorway wearing a more pleasant face and walked back to his spot in front of the mirrors. He picked up his comb and scissors and started trimming again as he said, "Jackson says you're a good egg. So I'm glad to help if I can, Mr. Nayland."

I looked at his reflection in the mirror. "I'm not really sure where to start at this point. But let me tell you a hypothetical story. Say there's a woman who has recently spent some private time with a man of another race. The knowledge of which would greatly offend her family and friends. Let me also suggest that there's a group, possible known by some as Alabama Nightriders, who would in the course of their fraternal business come upon this knowledge." I hesitated momentarily checking Flattens response. He remained pleasant, so I continued. "Would you happen to know anything about such a group?"

He held his tongue as he continued trimming my hair, but his eyes told me he was the type who couldn't resist weaving a good yarn. "You're asking if I know anything about that old southern secret society of misfits known as the Ku Klux Klan?"

I nodded as he asked seriously, "Are you afraid of the Ku Klux Klan, Mr. Nayland?"

"No more than any other ghost story," I replied.

"You by chance don't happen to belong to that particular order, do you, Mr. Nayland?"

I think he was going to call it something else, but from the twitch of his eye I noticed in his reflection that he had reservations in proceeding, either that or he really did fear the Klan.

I crossed my legs, trying to give the impression of calm. "No, I don't belong to any order, and like most of my fellow Americans, I prefer to play it alone. That's why I've never fallen for the allure of being a joiner."

Flatten seemed to take comfort from my statement and continued trimming as he spoke. "Glad to hear that, but too many others in this country don't seem to possess your practicality, Mr. Nayland."

My growing impression of this "friendly" barber was that he appeared to think that half the country belonged to the invisible empire and the other half went around in fear of it. I continued by asking if he was a member.

He almost laughed out loud. "Not me." He shook his head excitedly. "It's not the type of organization a good Irish boy should find himself in."

"That being true, what can you tell me about them?"

"Best as I can recall, the Klan inserted itself in the state back in 20s when a character by the name of George C. McCarren came up from Houston as the head Kleagle for the State of Oklahoma. That's the name for the Klan's membership recruiter. The story goes that the head office in Atlanta sent him up here to help Edward Y. Clark fill the chapters across the state. McCarren set up offices in Room 503 in the Baltimore Building, where he started to work with about twelve other recruiters covertly. McCarrren was a phenomenon particular to the land of free speech. He was a polarizing agent who could channel the energies of the nearly psychotic and the angry and the downtrodden who populate what we often call the lunatic fringe."

He stopped to spray some stray dry strands. "Anyway, McCarren and Clark recruited nearly seventy thousand members in those first few years and organized vigilante raids in the eastern part of the state. But after the riots and Governor Walton's impeachment, the organization speedily fell into disrepute. By '28 the Klan had become an unfrightening shell of its former self and as best as I can tell it has virtually ceased to exist here in the city, except for a few social outcasts that hang together for crime more than anything. Best I can pick up, only a few remaining active members exist, mostly up around Tulsa." When he finished, he pressed his lips together in comical disapproval.

I nodded my appreciation and asked him, "Say a man had to get to know these fellows to further a case he was working on. How would he join or better yet, how would a person need to act and appear to blend in?"

His memory seemed to lapse as he watched me for a moment, leaning against the counter. Then with a burst of enthusiasm he started in. "Well, you got to be white and American and a Protestant. You got to have klectoken, the ten-dollar initiation fee. If you have the ten the rest of it can be straightened out. You also need to have six-fifty for the old white robe. So it would cost an interested party sixteen-fifty all together to gain full entrance into the order. The members are not called brothers or anything like that. They call themselves citizens. The initiation is called being naturalized. They call non-member aliens."

"In the oath, the new citizen swears never to tell anything nor give evidence against a Klansman unless he's committed rape, willful murder or treason. But they welcome burglars, counterfeiters, drunks, and other felons. Hell, arsonists might be appreciated too—but I don't know on that."

He looked like he had more, but I interrupted him and asked about passwords and their greetings.

I sat silently waiting until a relaxed look came over his face and he opened up with a string of monikers of various Klansmen. There was the Exulted Grand Cyclops, Grand Dragon, Grand Wizard, the Klaliff, Klokann, Klabee, Kludd, Kloran, and Nighthawks and a host of others that I did not follow. All, he explained were elected by dens identified as Ghouls. I just listened and hoped that I had hair left as he combed and snipped.

As he continued with his story, he became more and more animated and snipped away with abandon as he went on to explain there was a secret grip or handshake that members used when they encounter one another. He described it as a shake with the left hand followed by a salute, of which I took careful note. He explained the salute had been copped from the Confederate army and is made by placing the right hand over the right eye and then turning the hand so the palm is facing the front. I looked into the mirror and tried to replicate the salute.

"Anything else I should know?" I inquired.

"There's a grip, whereby you shake a fellow member with an extended left hand. That's about it," he said with the dying excitement of a storyteller at the end of his tale. "You're not planning to get that close to any of those fellows in your investigation?"

"No. But I would like to be able to identify individuals connected to the Order to determine if they or their group have any bearing on my case."

He continued trimming. "Well, there's one important thing you should remember," he pointed his scissors at me in the mirror, "when you meet another Klansman you always say, AYAK."

"AYAK?" I repeated.

He snickered. "Are You a Klansman? If a guy pulls that line on you, remember to respond AKIA meaning, 'A Klansman I Am.' To be honest, the rest of the junk the boys can't remember due to the fact most aren't very bright. But those two principle things you should know to get by."

He showed me a cheap little celluloid button, explaining that they wear it wrong end out on the label of their coats. When he turned it, I noticed the letters spelled KOTOP Knights of The Open Palm. I took a good look at the back of that button. I couldn't take anything else from it, but I knew I would keep my eyes open for any gentleman displaying a decoration that way.

My quick lesson in the Klan was finished as he took out his electric clippers and sheared the back of my neck. When he removed the white bib and started dusting talc on the collar of my neck, I asked a direct question. "Can you tell me if Lawrence Davis or his son Brock is a member of a local chapter?"

He looked at me through the reflection of the mirror while asking, "You mean that old Oily that made all his money off the Indians up north?"

"That's the one," I said.

"No. Not that I know of. However, people in the know could get the impression the old man sure has sympathies that lie in that direction. But no, I've never heard gossip nor tales that either are members. But if you want, I can check into it and get back with you."

I gave an appreciative nod and my number. "Call me if you learn or think of anything else." As I walked over to retrieve my hat, I asked, "Dave, do you ever play the numbers?"

"Sometimes, why?"

"What was the number yesterday?"

"Let's see, I think a six was the first number...yes, I recall now, it was 615. You have anything down?"

"I think I did," I said with a grin before giving him five dollars. "And thanks for the cut as well as the information."

Flatten looked at the fin. "You're a class act, Nayland. It's a pleasure doing business with you. You come see me anytime."

120

Though Flatten's story had been informative, I couldn't piece together how any of it might be connected to Lauren's case, but reserved the thought that it might yet. I made the bell jingle as I walked out of the barbershop toward my car.

Chapter Eighteen

I dug into my coat pocket for my keys just as two mountainous men walked up on and placed their dirty hands under each of my elbows and stood me up straight. I turned my head side to side and noted that they both were wearing oil-covered bib overalls with sweat matted shirts underneath, which they wore with sleeves rolled up over their elbows.

The one on the right had a chaw of tobacco in his cheek, the juice of which had left a brown trail from the corner of his mouth down his chin. Each was adorned with leather, steel-toed boots caked in oil sludge along with steel hard-hats, off which the afternoon sun shone and briefly blinded me. I considered making a run for it, but I thought I'd have as much chance as a three-legged mule in a through-bred race in out running these two, so I let them hold me there next to my coupe.

A broad-shouldered man with dark hair approached from the corner of the building and stood next to our compact group at the curb. He was a foot wider and a head taller than I and possessed a disarming grin on his face. His smile was neither a greeting nor an emotion that I could respond to. It was the blind grimace of a man who lived in a world he owned, a world that didn't include me. He was dressed similarly to my two new escorts, except his clothes were spotless and the legs in his trousers both had a perfect pleats ironed down the center.

He stood with his string bean legs planted wide apart, peering at me out of coal-black eyes. Their whites were yellowish from some internal complaint: bad digestion or bad conscience. "Mr. Nayland, someone would like to speak to you. I suggest you come with us."

I guessed he was the tool pusher and in charge of this little gang of oil thugs. The two roughnecks pushed me across the street to a pickup truck.

The boss stated calmly, "Slide in, Mr. Nayland."

I felt the newly cut short hairs bristling on the back of my neck. I bowed my back, but the two roughnecks lifted me off the ground, when the squatter of the two said, "You heard what my friend said?"

I tried to keep my instincts out of my voice. "Have you got room?"

The talker shook his head and said, "You're a very funny man. I wanna keep you with me all the time, to make me laugh when I'm blue. Now get in."

I didn't move so the man in overalls opened the door and shoved me so hard I nearly bounced against the other side of the truck. I slid into the middle of the front bench seat. The boss followed me in and sat squarely in the passenger seat while the larger of the two roughnecks piled in behind the wheel. The other jumped into the bed of the truck. We drove off towards downtown.

For a moment I thought of the things I'd heard about people who were "taken for a ride." Then I tried to dispel the vague feeling of uneasiness by cold logic. These men were just roughnecks as I tried to convince myself that I must cease letting my imagination run away with its self.

At the tool pusher's direction, we pulled into a vacant parking space in front of the Petroleum Building on Third Street. The imported marble terracotta trimmed building, built eight years ago, and housed most of the major oil companies within its eighteen stories. At the top was the private dining club, aptly named The Petroleum Club.

The mountain in the back of the truck jumped out and opened the passenger side door. His hulking partner stepped out as they both reached in and pulled me out onto the sidewalk and escorted me through the double brass doors, with the tool pusher taking up the rear.

Our negligible group of misplaced misfits walked across the marble floor towards the elevators. The rig-hounds' steel-toed boots clicked onto the black marble like the tap dancing stars down in the Deuce. The elevator doors slid into the walls and we stepped in and rode the lift eighteen floors to the top.

Our little foursome stepped out onto luxuriously piled red carpet that covered the floor of the expensive-looking restaurant. The establishment was completely empty, except for two gentlemen seated at a large oak dinner table under a window looking out over the city. My escorts held me where we had stepped off, waiting for an unperceivable signal to proceed. I couldn't make out the man whose back we were now facing, but I could clearly see that the other was an older man wearing a perfectly tailored black suit and was pointing his finger at his guest and speaking in an agitated voice. Though I couldn't make out their conversation, the younger one was clearly being chewed out. After roughly five minutes, the guest stood up and walked towards us.

He gave me a stainless-steel look. I instantly recognized the young man. It was my new friend from the ballpark, Jersey Boy, and as he neared our party he spoke.

"Having a good day, Shamus?" He smirked.

"Better than most," I replied. "And better than yours, it appears. Were you getting your ears peeled back over there?"

His face turned blotchy red as he changed direction, puffed himself up in front of me. "I bet yours is going to get a hell of a lot worse, gumshoe," and then chortled, "Abyssinia, gumshoe."

"See ya in the funny papers, kid," I replied.

As the brass doors closed, my accompanists pushed me forward toward the old man. He was a man of distinguished appearance, correctly dressed, and well-groomed in the way of good living. His graying hair combed sharply, and a cleanly shaved face below a set of gold-rimmed glasses would have been at home on any portrait of a bank president. He didn't rise as I came up, but just pointed at the chair placed on the opposite side of the table. "Have a seat, Mr. Nayland."

"Do you know who I am?" he inquired. His voice was low, dry and monotonous, the voice of vicious boredom. It affected me like a rattlesnake's buzzing signal. I shook my head that I didn't.

"Well then, let me introduce myself. I'm Lawrence Davis." He looked me over with aesthetic distance. I didn't reply, but sat silently to see where this conversation might be going. His narrow slits eyes with the come hither look of a king cobra never left. We both sat there in silence. A waiter dressed in French attire came out of the swinging kitchen door and placed a twenty-ounce steak in front of Mr. Davis. As he cut into the medium rare steak, he spoke softly.

"Well, let's get down to business. It has come to my attention that you were a guest in my residence recently."

"By whom?" I inquired.

"That's really not important," he stated flatly as he took a bite of the pink steak. "I have since learned that you were there as a guest of my granddaughters and as a friend of her ne'er-do-well husband." He took another bite along with a sip of red wine as I spoke.

"I'm not sure what the problem is then, sir."

He looked down a thin nose at me with intellectual distaste. "I'm sure you don't see a problem. You wouldn't. So I'll spell it out for you. I've learned that you were introduced to my wife under false pretenses as a baseball scout or something or another not very productive to society. Unfortunately for you, I've discovered you're in fact a cheap keyhole peeping detective, but in fairness, it was stated that you're among the more intelligent, persistent members of your so-called profession."

I nearly let the yakker of a compliment go by, but like in my playing days, I couldn't lay off. "That was nice of whoever," I said with a smirk.

He now appeared to get more agitated as he spoke. "So my current concern is what a cheap gumshoe is doing sniffing around my family's home."

I sat in silence as the slow machinery in my head tackled the best way to extricate myself from this conversation without betraying Lauren.

"Care to enlighten me, Mr. Nayland?"

"I don't know. Maybe I'm just a baseball fan and really friends with Lauren and Johnny, and I didn't want to make your wife uncomfortable with my real profession."

"You're an Ananias liar." His voice rose like the front of a thunderstorm as he shuddered on the verge of fury.

"Calm down, Mr. Davis, because I don't have any damn answers for you at this time," I remarked in truth.

"No need to be course and vulgar, Mr. Nayland," the old man said in a different voice. "Look, Nayland, I'm a busy man and I don't need your type snooping around. It delights my competitors and makes my associates uneasy."

He went silent momentarily and then declared, "It's apparent to me now that my granddaughter has hired you to investigate some mischief in our family and if I were to guess, I would say it's most likely connected to that supposed professional baseball player of husband of hers." He grabbed the table with both hands, but maintained an air of calmness. "It doesn't matter."

His eyes hardened, gleaming like the lights in the ballpark in September. "I have my own means of keeping an eye on that so-called baseball player and keeping him out of trouble, or at least the papers. So my advice to you is to go back to my granddaughter and tell her you haven't found anything and the case is closed."

He relaxed his grip on the table as he asserted. "I would further add that if you do so, I would be inclined to provide you with a $500 bonus at such time." He let loose the table and looked down as he used his knife and fork to commit ritual murder upon his steak and quipped, "I think we understand one another, so good day to you, Mr. Nayland!"

I looked around for my oilfield escorts. They were sitting at another table drinking and didn't give the appearance of having any inclinations to assist me back to the elevator. So I stood up, thanked Mr. Davis for his time, and headed toward the elevator doors, but not feeling all that satisfied with myself. I stopped and looked the old man straight in the eyes, raised my right hand and placed it over my right eye, palm out, giving him the Klan salute as I spoke. "AYAK?"

He looked at me, momentarily confused, then he huffed and bristled, trying to recapture his anger without success. His voice was flat. "What's that, some guinea curse your landlady taught you?"

He pulled a cigar from a box on the table, looked at the band, cut it off with a nickel plated cigar cutter, and reached for his lighter as he told me. "Get the HELL out of here before I change my mind what to do with you,

Mr. Nayland."

As I rode the elevator down, I kept wondering what I'd done with the cereal, for I felt I was acting like a junior G-Man with a box-top badge. That thought faded as the riggings in my head tried to discern what the distinguished Mr. Davis really wanted and how much he really knew. I started to resent this case and hoped any and all future cases didn't involve dames.

I shrugged, thinking to myself, *Clever crime detection is one-third luck, one-third hard work, and one-third* intuition *~~institution~~. PI's like myself rated luck and intuition as a standoff which is to say one is as important as the other. I was always willing to work hard, and I knew that my intuition had stood me in good stead before and my intuition now told me that Davis's non-plus response likely eliminated the Klan or his use of the same as the blackmailer behind the letters. It also told me that blackmailing a woman really wasn't the Klan's or her father's style. Intuition also told me that if it had been the Klan, they would have simply moved against Timons directly in a much more sinister fashion.*

I hadn't penetrated any of the dark secrets surrounding the case, nor come to any conclusions to who was really behind the blackmailing of Mrs. Camp. I stepped out of the building into the oppressive summer heat. It struck me like a slap across the eyes. The streets were like an oven as the taxi arrived back at Flatten's and I still hadn't answered any of the questions circling within my head. I knew I needed to put in some real detective work and acquire a little luck to solve this case now.

Chapter Nineteen

L ater that Thursday, an undistinguished, pale young man lifted his foot from the gas pedal and slowed his blue, two-door Nash as he headed south along Robinson Avenue. Brock Davis neared the North Canadian as he pulled off onto a gravel road that ran parallel to the north river bank. The sun had fallen behind the lip of the horizon by then, and the western sky was scrawled like a childish finger-painting of colored cirrus clouds. Twilight flowed like a lighting-bug over the iron-stained river.

Beyond the reach of the car's headlights stood a large, poled-canvas tent glowing eerily in the southern night. The lights of the tent reflected off the slow moving water as it rolled on southward. The young driver noticed there were already hundreds of cars parked around the revival tent with lines of people strolling into the large openings. The women wore light, cool cotton summer dresses in shades of cream and white, with light, little summer hats with colored ribbons wrapped around the brim and flowing down their backs. Many had on their cleanest overalls and clean, cotton button-down shirts. No matter their apparel, all the men were clean shaven. Not even the poorest, which represented the largest number in the crowd, showed up dirty for a meeting with the Lord.

Brock pulled his coupe up to the end of a line of cars, stepped out and locked the door. It was hot, even though the sun was nearly down. The pale driver liked the heat. It reminded the masses hell existed. A reminder, he believed, the weakened masses of the nation required. He loosened his silk scarf from around his neck, turned up his shirt collar and pressed his white straw hat firmly upon his head.

Brock stood back from the growing crowd and observed that the area around the tent had a circus-like atmosphere. Children escaped the grips of their mothers. Neighbors chatted with one another. He heard some going on about the dust that had covered the city from Tuesday's 'Black Roller.' The young man never understood why there wasn't more discipline and reverence. He stood judging their sin-filled hearts for their lack of respect to be in the presence of Sister Aimee. He knew they were all liars and thieves. They performed wicked acts daily with their lustful transgressions and immoral ways. He started feeling anxious and his heart began to race as he contemplated being in the tent with the blessed Pentecostal evangelist, Sister Aimee.

Brock watched the crowd shuffle in, preferring to observe crowds rather than join them. Sweat dripped down his face, making his cheaters slide slightly down to the tip of his nose. He pushed them up with his middle finger, removed his straw hat and ran his left hand over his blonde, slicked-back hair. He slowly made his way to the illuminated tent.

Brock quickly slipped into the nearest line and bumped and cut his way into the tent. Once inside, he saw the rows of wooden planks set off the ground before a raised, curtained stage. The platform had a solitary microphone set in the middle of the stage with four large round speakers cabled to the posts directed out into the audience. To the left a small orchestra appeared ready to start the show. The seats before the orchestra were filled with fellow whites while colored members of the community filled in the back. Though Sister Aimee preached to all, segregation crept into the Foursquare Church. Brock, with his thin features, frowned at such tolerance as he forced himself into an unoccupied seat near the front of the main center aisle, but as far away from a large family with children as was possible. He scanned the hall but failed to recognize me sitting beneath my fedora and turned-up collar across the large enclosure.

The man sitting to Brock's right was clearly a farmer, dressed in overalls and boots. Sweat dripped from his temples. He held the Gospel in his hand. A small crowd pushed into the tent to grab the remaining empty seats, but it appeared there were still hundreds waiting outside. Signs were posted around the tent calling for all to join the righteous and be healed of their sinful ways.

A small man in a brown woolen suit approached the microphone and whistled into it, gaining everyone's attention.

"Please be seated," he commanded, "or Sister Aimee can't begin."

As he walked off the stage, the orchestra began to play "America the Beautiful." Suddenly a dozen white-robed choir singers appeared on the right side of the platform and began singing the lyrics. The farmer and the woman in the yellow dress began to sing at the top of their lungs. Both appeared to be tone deaf, but immune to the judgmental looks they received from those around them. When the song concluded, the musicians and the choir led straight into "This Land is Your Land." The whole congregation stood and continued to follow, song after song. In between songs they shouted thanks to the Lord, the Nation and Sister Aimee. They remained standing and continued to sing as the band began "God Bless America."

As the music faded away, anticipation and sweat filled the tent. The curtains on the stage swung open and actors dressed as the "Pilgrim Fathers" stepped onto the stage to rousing applause. They reenacted the landing of the Mayflower at Plymouth Rock and proclaimed the new nation's foundation on conservative Christian ideals. The young man rose from his seat at the conclusion of the play and applauded enthusiastically. The Founding Fathers played out the drawing up of the constitution, a document they declared "conceived in prayer and executed by Christian gentlemen." The third scene featured Abraham Lincoln on his knees in prayer, "Seeking guidance of his God in the times of national stress," proclaiming that, "without a doubt, the Protestant God had blessed the United States."

Brock watched as the actors played out the fall of harmonious Christian America as its citizens began to strive to be modern by removing the Bible from schools, embraced the concept of biological evolution, turned away from old time religion and tried to blot out God, who had protected our great nation. He could feel the anger rise from within as he, too, saw every day how God was being pushed out of his life, as well as those close to him. As he sat with clinched fists, the orchestra fell silent and a hush fell over the crowd. He tensed as those around him tensed. A new actor appeared on stage. The villain, an atheist and a communist, took a hammer and chisel to an oversized dollar bill, chipping away the words "In God We Trust." He walked to the far side of the stage and using red paint, spattered over the word "God" in an enlarged copy of the national anthem. The man stood and the whole crowd gasped in horror. The villain continued. When the capital building appeared, he replaced the stars and stripes with a red communist flag. Just as it appeared the villain completely undermined the United States, to the stage stepped a stunning woman dressed entirely in white—Sister Aimee Semple McPherson. The young howled with excitement and the remaining crowd went wild, cheering and screaming for the radiant cultural icon who would save those attending, and America, as well.

McPherson smiled and bowed. She addressed the crowd in a high-pitched nasal strained singsong voice. "America! Awake! The enemy is at our gates! They are penetrating our walls! America! You are in danger! An enemy power is penetrating our strongholds! There is death in their hands-the bombs of atheism and of communism and anarchy! America! Awake! Defend your own!"

Uncle Sam jumped onto the stage, sprinted forward and grabbed the villain and issued him a ticket back to Russia. The young man was almost in tears as he cheered for Sister Aimee and America. McPherson strode across the stage and tore down the red flag flying over the stage prop Capital and replaced it with the stars and stripes. The whole congregation, including the thin featured young man, erupted in applause. Thanks to Sister Aimee, the nation and its Christian foundation are saved.

McPherson held her hands high and spoke to the standing crowd. "With God, I can do things! But with God and you, and the people who you can interest, and by the grace of God, we're gonna cover the World...withhold, time, religion and the goodness of our America."

Brock and the whole audience were on their feet cheering for Sister Aimee. The orchestra struck up "God Bless America." As Sister Aimee walked into the crowd, she touched the outstretched hands of her followers. As she eventually came down the aisle where the young man was sitting, the young man reached out as she passed. Her hand suddenly clasped his out reached fingers.

Sister Aimee spoke aloud. "Faith without works is like a bird without wings." As Sister Aimee neared the exit, she turned back to the congregation and declared. "We are all making a crown for Jesus out of these daily lives of ours, either a crown of golden, divine love, studded with gems of sacrifice and adoration, or a thorny crown, filled with the cruel briars of unbelief, or selfishness, and...lustful sin."

I watched the strange interaction between Sister Aimee and Brock. He seemed to be bursting with excitement. After Mrs. McPherson's final declaration, the young professor weaved into the crowd and rushed outside.

Chapter Twenty

I t was a hot, sweaty, Saturday night as Lesley slipped out of Lauren's fifth-floor apartment in the Mayfair and headed towards the back staircase. His perfectly polished loafers disappeared into the thick, sage-green rug with alternating rose blooms woven into its pattern. Without realizing it, he began to place his tan wingtips on each bloom, consciously avoiding stepping on the sage-green outlines, like a small girl playing hopscotch. He noticed that someone had left open a window, allowing a pleasant summer breeze to drift swiftly down the hall and main front stairwell. It cooled him briefly, but the sapping heat still remained in the building. At the top of the rear stairwell, he looked over and tilted his left ear downward in an attempt to determine if anyone was returning home via the rear stairs. Hearing and seeing nothing, he quickly took the five flights of stairs down to the large metal security door that took him into the back ally where he had left his uncle's hearse.

The red exit light flickered over his head as he popped the steel cross lever, opening the security door. He cautiously glanced both ways and stepped out into the warm Oklahoma night. A single white security bulb wrapped in a gray metal hood shown down onto his shoulders as he stood there. He turned his wrist up to check the time, 11:50. Looking up into the western sky, he could clearly pick out the three stars of Orion's belt twinkle in a vertical pattern above Venus. Most of the city lights were turned off or dimmed so he could make out the lesser four stars that composed Orion's bow. As he stared up at the summer sky, he dug into his suit pocket, pulled out a pack of Lucky Strikes and a gold plated lighter. He turned his back to the wind, cupping the lighter inside his other in an attempt to light the cigarette. He failed to notice the man with the long face slouched against the outside of the building, in the shadows, like a marionette with no strings attached.

The tip of the cigarette glowed red into the young dark handsome man's face. The hidden interloper's hand flicked into a pocket and came out with a polished, heavy leather device that resembled a pear. He swung the sap in a wide sweeping motion, moving it fast enough that Timons couldn't avoid it. The heavy sap hit Timons squarely on the back of the neck, just below his hairline. He went down like one of those cows zapped on the meat processing line in cow-town.

A quiet stillness hung in the night air as the dark figure quickly walked over to his two-door sedan and jumped in. He backed the car up till the trunk compartment opened up directly over the unconscious form. The shadowy figure quickly bound the senseless Timons' hands and feet with a thick brown hemp rope. He lifted the unconscious body into the trunk. It took one final lift to put the stupefied man's trailing legs completely in the rear compartment. He slammed the trunk shut. Checking up and down the alley way to make sure he was still in the clear. He jumped into the still running sedan and rapidly drove up the alley way, turning west when he reached 13th Street and out of the city.

Chapter Twenty-One

The following morning was still and quiet, that kind of quiet stillness that comes just before sunrise. It was the stiff quietness that you feel. But on this particular Sunday the calmness was abruptly shattered by the screaming telephone.

I'd been on a surveillance job for a divorce client, staked outside a cheap hotel out on Highway 81. Waiting for a cheating husband to appear at, or in, the room of a local working girl. Neither of the pair ever showed, and it was pushing two a.m. before I got in. So I was tired, dead tired when the phone screamed at me again. I didn't do anything about the annoying vibrating black bake-lit box. I rolled over and tried to swim back down into the sticky honey of sleep and wished whoever was calling would give up.

The phone rang sharply again. I lay wide awake in the darkness, knowing going back to sleep in that hot, muggy morning was out of the question. The bed springs creaked as I placed my feet on the cool wood floor. The fourth ring stretched through the darkness of my apartment. I looked down at the Hamilton on my wrist. The radium-painted dial told me it was 5:20. I'm not good in the morning, especially not a hot, humid one. I walked out of the bedroom towards the phone. The black horn rang again. Muttering to myself, "If it's that damn important, they'll let it ring until I pick up." I kicked the end table, making the small onion shaped lamp fall off on my foot. "Shit."

The phone rang again. "All right, I'm coming!" I picked up the receiver. "What?"

"Hello, Lou." A strong southern voice came over the horn.

"Yeah."

The voice at the other end spurted out something about "found" and "dead" in a sharp and authoritative tone, but I didn't understand what he said. Mostly I was still asleep and second, I had dropped the phone. I picked up the receiver.

"Say what again…dead…who's dead?"

Slowly the fog between my ears cleared, and I recognized the voice. "Jackson, this really you? Really…damn it. No…where…?"

Seconds ticked away. "Give me thirty minutes to put my shoes on and get out that way."

I needed coffee first, so I trudged out to my tiny cubicle of a kitchen. I lit a burner and placed yesterday's stale pot of Joe on the back of the stove.

On a towel rack above the stove, a pair of dark cotton socks hung limply. I took them down and stretched them out in my hands. They were clean, size ten and half—I had washed and hung them up to dry the night before. Nearly dry, so I threw them over my shoulder and went back to my bedroom to grab my smokes.

I returned to the kitchen and sat at the white-enamel top kitchen table and reached for the aspirin bottle sitting on the table. The bottle originally had fifty tablets and still contained fourteen. I dumped three on the table and pulled out a cigarette. I slowly rolled it back and forth between my forefinger and my thumb, thinking. What could Jackson want with me at 5:00 AM on a Sunday morning? Couldn't be any of my current cases, most were all but completed and I hadn't really pushed anybody's button yet in the Camp case. But he sees me connected to something, either intentionally or accidently, and he wants answers. I picked up the nickel lighter from the counter, manipulated it, and lit the cigarette in the corner of my mouth. I sat there in my pajama pants, shirtless, waiting for the coffee to boil. When the pot steamed, I poured a cup, swallowed the three aspirin, washing them down with the hot Joe, and headed back to the bedroom.

I ran my fingers through my hair, scratched the back of my neck and began putting on my white union suit, a pair of socks and the pants from my gray suit. I had no choice. I had two suits, and I'd lived in the brown one for the last three days, so the gray one won the toss. When I had fastened my shoes,

I returned to the kitchen for another cup of battery acid. Upon my return I put on a light gray and pink thinly striped shirt, Irene's gift to me on my birthday. The dry cleaners always left the collar soft when they starched the rest. I finished with a solid, woven gray tie. I stuffed the pack of cigarettes, keys, money and wallet with my PI license into my pockets and quietly shut the front door.

I sluggishly pulled out my car keys, unlocked the door and got in just as the first light of the day crept over the eastern horizon. The orange rays of sunlight beamed across the dashboard as I pulled out and headed west as fast as the law allowed, pondering the ironic idea. "Of being flattered that Jackson had called me in on a consultation." A smirked erupted on my lips.

Jackson said he would be waiting for me next to the pavilion on the north side of Lake Overholser. The lake had been built back in teens to provide water for the city. The large flat lake barely reached a depth of seven feet except near the dam. It wasn't the kind of place someone would try to hide ill deeds. The lake lay adjacent to Route 66 on the edge of the small Nazarene town of Bethany. "The Mother Road" ran directly through the main street of the sleepy little burgh and parallel to the lake on its way to Los Angeles.

The betting odds were poor that whatever Jackson had found had anything to with any of the cases I was working on, but the thing about the law of averages is, it never works. Oh, it works in the terms of the daily numbers game, you'll never win that. But in terms of anything practical, the law averages simply hasn't a chance.

I murdered scores of insects on the fifteen mile stretch of road between my apartment and the lake. Nearing the lake, I pulled off highway at the spot where two sheriff cars were parked next to the reservoir. Their headlights were shining out onto the water. A small breeze blew out of the southwest causing white caps to lap up against the shore where I noticed a group of men holding flashlights.

I parked behind the deputy sheriff's prowler parked next to a large, silver Packard sedan. I knew it belonged to the poor bastard who was doing his weekly shift as the county medical examiner. Oklahoma County did not employ a full-time, formal medical examiner, but rather depended on local physicians who volunteered to take one or two weeks each year in this capacity. Whoever it was this week had drawn the short straw now had the bad fortune to be called out early on a Sunday morning.

Approaching the circle of men holding flashlights, I observed some of the usual suspects. Tom Miller, a towheaded youngster of twenty-five, with all the nerve in the world, and Al Croak, both sheriff deputies who were both pointing their service lights on a large object lying at the side of the lake.

The glare of their flashlights lanced the darkness off the scowling face of Under-Sheriff under his wide-brimmed hat. He stood over a man bent over a large dark object sprawled out on the edge of the water. Jackson had his Stetson tilted back from his brow as he stood staring down at the blue lump of a dead man. He appeared to be asking questions of the man kneeled on the ground before him. He stood there with both hands on his hips. His posture caused the flaps of his tan Filson waist coat to pull apart and spread back behind his large hands on his hips. Allowed the service lights to reflect off his large ivory handle .45 Long Colt stuck in an engraved leather holster on his right hip.

When I came closer, I heard a low rhythmic tenor voice roll towards me...

The Lord is my shepherd, I lack nothing
He makes me lie down in green pastures,
He leads me beside quiet waters...

Even though I walk through the darkest valley,
I will fear no evil...

Deputy Miller's voice faded over the body of the lake as I snapped an old willow branch strewn across the walking trail. I continued on and came to a stop next to the dark party.

My nose twitched suddenly as the distinct bitter scent of death seeped into my nostrils. Attempting to distant myself from the smell, I stepped closer to where Jackson stood and asked, "How's business for the master criminologist this morning?"

"Abundant!" He replied as he tucked a black enameled evidence case under his left arm. He held it pressed under there as if it was full of jewels.

A tough PI is supposed to joke in the face of death, I'm not that tough, but I try to pretend. "What's the word on your new friend here?"

"It appears he's gone to sit on the right hand of God, if God don't mind the fella's got a bullet hole," he remarked with uncharacteristic humor. The two young deputies exchanged swift glances at each other, not sure how to react to their boss's attempt at humor.

I was used to Brice's feeble attempts at humor, so I just asked the group as a whole, "Who found the body?"

With a solemn and composed face he stated, "A city water worker checking the spillway called it in."

"Nobody saw anything suspicious?" I probed.

"This far from town?" Brice injected.

I nodded as casual a nod as on the street. "Know who killed him?"

Jackson scowled, tilted his Stetson up while looking down at the corpse and with the dryness of the surrounding prairie grass exclaimed. "I would guess someone with a gun!"

I shook my head to myself. If he needed my help, I needed some information, not his dry-ass prairie wit. I was tired, and it was too early in the day for our usual bullshit back and forth. He handed the evidence case to Deputy Miller and reached into his jacket pocket and pulled out a small silver flask, took a swig and stated. "Damn, it's damp next to the water. Care for a drink, Lou?" That being about as close as Brice comes to being chummy.

"Only when I can get it," I replied.

I took a swig and then handed the flask back to Jackson as I recognized Doc Steve Rowell, business-like and outwardly unmoved, bent over what was clearly the body of a well-built, colored man in his late twenties dressed in a slate blue suit. Doc himself was a medium built man with strong lean physical features. City legend had it he possessed the hands and fingers of a great virtuoso, both on the piano and in surgery. It was also said, mostly in much seedier circles and within law enforcement, that he was the man to see if you accidently acquired a gunshot wound and hoped to see the sunrise again, but at a reasonable price.

I looked down at the lifeless body, which appeared untouched, though the clothes were rumpled and twisted. His legs were close together, one atop of the other. His left arm lay fallen over his belt while his right arm was jetting straight into the water, palm up, with rigid fingers curled around a blue floral silk handkerchief. I noticed a blood baked bruise at the base of his skull as well as the drying blood seeping from a wound in his chest which in a star-like pattern, the edges of which stained his pin-striped suit. His head was tilted to the side, which forced his eyes to stare out onto the lake. They were frozen open in a death stare. The subsequent signs of death were already appearing as a fine white film had started to form over his once pure brown eyes.

I leaned back on my heels. "I assume death by lead poisoning?"

Brice looked right at me. "Smartasses like yourself can read about it like everyone else in the afternoon paper, if you're lucky."

The medical examiner pumped air out of his lungs in a short laugh which had no sound except the sound made by the air passing his teeth and nostrils.

With quick competence he examined the body and stated, "One bullet wound. Shot straight through the pump. The hole appears to be from a small caliber auto, most likely a .32, one of those small guns that fit so nicely into a woman's purse. But I can't be sure until I dig out the slug and you find a gun so I can run some ballistics," he said to us as a whole in a calm, detached manner.

When Doc pushed his metallic probe into the wound, I caught the acrid odor of recently expended smokeless powder and stepped back. Giving me a look that suggested I should step back further, he finished his analysis and then spoke professionally. "The powder burns suggest it occurred point blank."

Jackson asked, "How long ago?"

"Seven, maybe eight hours, sometime just after sunset last night, anyway. But there's something unusual you should see before you run off." Deputy Croak was trying to keep up and take down everything Dr. Rowell explained in a little red note pad.

The doc pointed at the victim's mouth, waiting for the nearest deputy to put a beam of light on it from his service light. The mouth was filled with dry crimson blood, which had also been coughed out onto the ground in the poor soul's last minutes of life.

Brice said, "So, plenty of gunshot victims cough up blood."

Doc shook his head as he used his long metal probe to open the man's mouth. "This one has lost his tongue. It appears from the bleeding it was before he died. And look at this," he said in a soft, even voice as he pulled up the sleeve on the victim's right arm. Around the wrist red welted ligature marks clearly stood out.

Brice listened attentively while the medical examiner explained, "My guess is that he was tied up like a spring steer before he was shot. Probably at some other location. It appears the body was dumped here after he was killed. There's not enough pooled blood under the body." He tilted the body so those above could observe the ground beneath. "See, there's nearly none." As the words spilled off his lips, the county meat wagon pulled up.

The police photographer snapped shots of the dead Timons lying next to the water and of the blurred tire treads in the soft ground above the body; Jackson walked over and motioned me back toward the parked cars. When we were a good distance away from the men loading the corpse onto the cold, stainless gurney, he spoke.

"Sorry to bring you out here so early," Jackson said, his voice weary, "but I need to know, what's your involvement in this?"

"What makes you think I've got any?"

Brice's eyes flared. "Because of our lunch conversation and it's just the kind of cockeyed murder you'd have something to do with."

"Sorry, Holmes, but I've got nothing to do with this, nor do I think it's connected to my current case," I fibbed.

He shifted his weight to his other foot, scowled at me and then continued, "I hate wasting my time on these shine killings. No one in their community likes talking to the cops. Anyway, do you recognize the stiff?"

I debated in my head briefly how much I should give over to him, thinking I owed him to be mostly straight. "His name is Lesley Timons. He's a drummer for one of those jazz bands that play on the weekends down in the Deuce." I decide it might be best not to mention that I had met and spoke with Timons in my office just three days ago.

"Are you sure about that?" he asked. "Because it sure seems to me that's there more to this mess than shows on the surface. Whenever you—"

I cut him short. "I didn't put him under a magnifying glass. I just bumped into him briefly when I was checking out a lead down in the Deuce on Wednesday afternoon. It was only for a moment as he walked out of the Aldridge," I fudged. "So I have nothing for you on his background other than he plays the drums. He seemed to be a good egg though."

"You still sure this isn't connected to that case we spoke about at lunch?" he dug again.

"No, I have no reason to believe he is," I told him. I paused for a long moment and then added, "Like I said, it was only a brief introduction."

He stood quietly for a second and then stared at me. "This sure doesn't look like your style for busting your clients out of a tight situation."

I gave him a quick response, raising both my eyebrows. "I've said I had nothing to do with this!"

He smiled and raised a cigarette to his mouth just as the morning breeze whipped sparks from its red end. He dropped it into the red dirt and put it out with his cowboy boot before he asked.

"Either way, do you have any red points you can give me on who might have actually gone to such lengths to make his story die with him?"

I was honest. "No, but give me a couple of days."

There was an awkward interval before he took hold of my coat sleeve. "Look, Lou, just a passing thought. You sure you're not holding out on me? And you sure you don't want to play one and one makes two with me?" His faint accent lent flavor to the question.

"Yeah, yeah, I'm sure, Sheriff, and you've really got to stop being suspicious of everyone." I winked as I started to leave. "I'll see you around."

"Whoa, just wait a minute," he exclaimed as he turned a fish eye on me. "I know all about your professional ethics. You know relations between client and private detective, but, we won't go into that here." He hesitated briefly. "You know the law on many points is quite clear," he said, forgetting for once to indulge his wit.

"Clear like what, Sheriff?" I asked.

"Clear like the status of an accessory before or after the fact in a murder case, and like aiding and abetting a criminal. Like a lot of things you know all about." He paused as if expecting an answer, but getting none, plunged on. "Either way, if your memory returns, you come see me first."

"Okay, Brice. But this time I hope you'll conduct a decent investigation," I said teasingly. "Maybe Timons ended up here this morning because he was overdue on a book from the library."

He shook his head. "Get the hell out of here, you bum, before I run you in as a material witness."

Having already ruined my recent shoe-shine, I started back to my car while yelling back, "I'll see ya around."

I left Jackson and drove back to town considering the possibility that Cecelia may have killed Lesley out of jealousy, but rejected the idea just as quickly due in large to the fact that Timons had had his tongue cut out and had been tied up in such a professional manner for any woman to have done it. But you never know, I told myself. Women have been making fools of men since Eve opened the first fruit stand.

I let those thoughts whirl around my brain as I headed back to my apartment for a few more hours of sleep. I also decided it would best to call Lauren and break the news to her about Timons after I had a few more hours of shut eye.

Chapter Twenty-Two

I arrived back at my apartment shortly before sunrise and attempted to get a few more hours of shut-eye. However, the muggy summer air made breathing as laboring as sitting inside a Turkish bath. With my room on the ground floor facing nothing, I lay in bed in my damp shorts, sweating up my sheets. Turning over in search of the cool patch of the bed, I realized I wasn't going to nod back off. I sat up, and without bothering to put on slippers, stood erect. I quickly felt searing pain from the glory days past shoot down my arm. It made my stomach turn over, just like at the moment of the original injury. Though flushed I gave it a couple complete rotations, rubbed it and then stumbled into the tiny bathroom.

I hit the light, jumped in the shower and brushed my teeth, felt better after dabbing some after-shave lotion under my armpits and putting on fresh shorts. I stretched out on my couch and read the evening paper, starting backward from the sporting page.

There wasn't a damn thing in the paper: Thursday Night, Oklahoma Indians lose to Ft. Worth Felines when the team score eight more or less solid base knocks in the first inning. That concluded in nine to three win for the Cats, the Dodgers still have a mathematical chance of gaining the pennant. The comics weren't funny. There was a cheesecake picture of some lush babe asking for a divorce because her marriage was "kiss-less." A mild looking guy named Cole was accused of taking a bank for twenty-five thousand dollars with a toy gun, and Alfonso Torchelle, a member of the syndicate's High Table, was still barricaded in a Hot Springs hotel daring the authorities to boot him out, talking out of both sides of his mouth about

144

suing the City of Hot Springs for calling him a "gangster." There was a standard item about a Hollywood busted marriage "which will spill dirt all over the papers when it comes to court." The Front page had the usual story of a new gusher atop the Capitol Hill fields sprayed the city with dark liquid money for two consecutive days.

I tossed the paper on the floor and rolled back onto the damp pillows. Somehow the promised dirt never came out, and I wondered if the columnists ran these items when they were short of material. And a guy has to have more courage than people think to use a toy gun in a stick-up. But they were right about Torchelle, one of the unknown big shots. He was rapped once for assault with a dangerous weapon when he was seventeen, then dropped out of the gang picture till a Treasure Department informant spot lighted him as the pillar of posh New Orleans community, a son at Harvard, daughter at some finishing school named Wesley…and the holder of the purse strings of the biggest crime mob in the country.

The quiet of the room gave me the spooks. I rolled onto my back and looked up to the white square tiles laid out in perfect lines on my ceiling. My living room couch wasn't that soft, but the room had been cooler after my early morning shower. My small apartment comprised three little separate rooms, the bedroom and bath, the living room and a small kitchen. It was a bachelor hodgepodge, untouched by the human hand for weeks on end until my landlady insisted on coming in and doing something about it. Cooking utensils, stained shirts, and unwashed socks were scattered on the floor and furniture. There was an open bottle of scotch, half empty, on the kitchen table at the back of the room. A lone coffeepot sat on the rear burner of the stove, and dirty dishes were still in the sink. It would have been just another dingy room if it hadn't been for the black and white baseball photos hung on the wall. A stealthy knock on the front door crept across the apartment.

"Who is it?" I said.

Abruptly the voice of the sharp-nosed woman on the other side of the door said, "Mrs. Giannasi! It's a time to get up," she said as she used her passkey to enter. "You'ah never gunna catch 'no' early worm snoring your life away and besides, how do expect'ah me to clean your rooms with you'ah lying about like a slug?" Her voice trailed off in obscure Italian mumblings.

Still muttering, I stood up and put on a pair of pants and glared at my landlady. Mary Giannasi, a tough old Italian broad of indeterminate age, who wore black horn-rimmed glasses that failed to conceal her penetrating, dark-brown eyes under her flowing black hair streaked with strands of gray over her olive-colored face. She was a widow who had come over the pond aboard the SS Touraine after the Great War to live with distant cousins working the coal mines of Oklahoma when she married a Welsh carpenter. They built and ran the two-story brick apartment with six single-room units there on 11th Street where I lived. Her husband had been killed six years ago when he drove his Harley motorcycle under a parked Red Ball storage truck. After his death, she stayed and continued running the apartments.

The old gal was like a den mother that ran roughshod over the coyote pack of single males that were her tenants. Mostly the men all appreciated her hospitality and occasional mothering. I liked her too, but I was not amused with her early morning appearance.

"I've already had my morning walk around a city lake, come back later," I exclaimed. "And I got back here at 7:30 this morning, three hours before your damn knocking."

She just smiled over her glasses at me and asked, "Whatta you doing up at that'ah un-Godly hour? Did some poor'ah soul die?"

"Actually, someone did," I replied.

"Anyone I know?" she inquired.

"Not unless you know any colored jazz musicians," I replied

She gave me a devilish smile. "I know'ah lots of people, Mr. Nayland, and you'ah might be surprised who."

Her constant smile and youthful demeanor always prevented me from remaining too annoyed with her little antics. She was one of those rare birds who awoke each day with delight, no matter what curve balls life threw her way. So, I naturally smiled back.

"You'ah poor young man, you'ah had a bad night. Put'ah on some more clothes and I'll fix'ah an early lunch. You'ah look like you could'ah use it." Her mothering instincts were kicking in and I wasn't in the mood to dissuade her.

I headed back to the bathroom, shaved, put on a clean shirt and my other suit. When I arrived back in the kitchen, a plate of toasted bread covered with corned beef and gravy were awaiting me on the table. Mrs. Giannasi being an Old World lady never sat at my table unless I asked her.

She touched the top of my head with her worn hand as she walked out of the kitchen and picked up her vacuum cleaner and began to sweep the living room rug. I knew she would say a prayer for me later.

I finished my lunch and drank a second cup of coffee. The vacuum quit running and the old gal returned to the kitchen and placed my plates in the sink. But as she did so, I couldn't help noticing her usual upbeat expression had changed.

"Is there something on your mind this morning, Mrs. Giannasi?"

"Do you'ah knowa my younger sister, Menga?"

"No, I haven't had the pleasure," I replied.

She continued, "She'sah staying with me for a few weeks until she'ah can settle her monies. You'ah see her husband was killed last month on what you call a derrick. Now'ah she staying with me to save monies."

I looked up to the corner of the ceiling as a spider descended its silken line toward the top of the cupboards. I'd wondered where this conversation was leading. She usually was happy, but reserved, and only politely asked questions regarding my ongoing cases. I always believed I was like a criminal soap opera like on the radio for her. So when we both had time, she would seek little details on the people, places and crimes I was currently involved with, and rarely spoke about her or her large extended family.

I thought she possibly needed money for her sister, but in all the years I had lived under her roof she had never raised my rent or asked for an extra cent. But I made a supporting offer, anyway.

"I can pay my rent for next month's early if that would help you out."

She pushed the very thought away with an awkward sweep of her arm. "I thank you'ah, but I no need your monies long as I have the strength in me body to make'ah an honest living, the Lord knows I still do."

"Are you or your sister in trouble?" I asked as I pushed out the other kitchen chair for her to sit. "Please have a seat, Mrs. Giannasi."

She paused a moment, looking down at the worn black-and-white checkered floor, and then sat in the chair I had pushed out. She smoothed the pleats in her white and red cotton day dress and began.

"I'ma as fine as the healthy tomato in my garden Mr. Nayland and monies ain't my problem."

She hesitated for a long minute. "It'sa family issue. My'ah sister has'a learned her late husband may'ah have fathered a child with'a nother woman."

The final words left her lips as she unconsciously moved her un-manicured fingertips from the side of her nose to her high bronze cheekbones. "And'a you'ah see, Mr. Nayland, she'sa afraid to asked any'aone about it, but I'ah might've spoke of you'ah and your'ah wonderful stories about your'ah work. So she'ah wondering if you'ah could look into these things about'ah her husband and ah child."

I nodded in the affirmative as took a sip of hot coffee and said I would look into it.

One of the old lady's skeletal hands made a gesture. "That'ah be nice, Mr. Nayland. Thank you'ah, thank you'ah, your'ah wonderful." Then added with pride, "I would'ah pay'ah you for your time and expenses."

I took hold of her out-stretched hands. "That's not important. But you see, I'm still a little confused. What do you need, Mrs. Giannasi? Your sister's husband is dead, there doesn't seem to me to be anything gained by me confirming the rumors other than more sorrow for sister."

She smoothed another wrinkle in her dress. "Well'ah you see, if there is a child, she'ah wants to help the poor'ah young thing, if she'ah can." Her face flushed as she looked back at me.

"Oh, I see," I responded. "In that case, I would be happy to see what I could find out for you and your sister."

Mrs. Giannasi looked relieved. "Bless you'ah, Mr. Nayland, bless you'ah."

"Tell your sister that I'll look into it." She smiled and went over to retrieve her vacuum cleaner and scurried out of my apartment.

I thought over this Humpty-Dumpty situation. Even if Mrs. Giannasi had her facts straight, I doubted that a child existed, and if the child did exist, I doubted a few more days of me not finding him wouldn't change the child's circumstances much. I could spend a couple days on it after the Camp case concluded.

I walked to the coffee table as I got to thinking about Cole, who'd taken the bank with a toy rod. How did they know his name? I sat and picked up the paper, read the whole piece this time. Amateur crooks are as dumb as hell. Cole had been a depositor in the very bank he held up. By this time, the cops would have him for sure.

I flipped back to the sports section of the *Daily Oklahoman* and opened it to page fourteen to see what time the Indians were playing the Exporters. I noted in the League standings that the Indians had moved into first place, 70 wins and only 57 losses. The final pennant run would be tight. I suddenly got more excited about going to the game.

Chapter Twenty-Three

After eating lunch at the restaurant inside the Greyhound bus station, I headed toward Holland Field for the game. Rolling down the window, I suddenly remembered that I had forgotten to call Lauren regarding Timons' death, but figuring it wouldn't hit the newsstand until tomorrow, I decided I'd call her after the game. As I drove up to the field, I noticed the stunning Miss Cecelia May crossing the road from the parking lot to the right field bleachers. She was smartly dressed in a pale blue pants and a white blouse, identical to the one Katharine Hepburn worn in *Alice Adams*. I couldn't see her face because of the matching blue, brisk down-tilt sailor hat she wore pinned to her loose black curls. Respectability controlled the natural movements of her body and stiffened her back.

I knew it would be best if I told her myself that Lesley Timons had been murdered. I parked the green coupe behind the right field fence. I headed around the corner to see if Cecelia had an escort for today's game.

I looked through the cross-wired fence behind the right field stands. Being a Sunday afternoon, the bleacher seats were filled to capacity with the Second Street community. I stood on the gravel pathway looking upward into the crowd searching for the beautiful round face of Cecelia. A quiet hush fell over the raucous crowd. All eyes looked at me in that dead, alien silence of another race. The only sound to be heard was the repetitive cadence of the hot dog barker selling 5 cent dogs.

"Dogs! Get your hot dogs here!"

The crowd continued to stare down at me with a deep suspicion, rather than any animosity. Cecelia broke the spell when she waved over at me from the far left rail. I smiled, walked up the center stairs to the fifth row and excused myself politely to men and woman seated until I found myself sitting next to her. Her lips were stained a bright red for her afternoon outing, and her glamorous black curls glittered in the bright summer sun under her hat. The hat worked for her. I liked the girl under the hat too.

Cecelia extended her hand. "This is an unexpected surprise, Mr. Nayland."

Taking the soft extended fingers into my palm, I said, "Not really. I'm a huge baseball fan."

I looked straight at her, and her female companion who looked to be a girl of twenty. Cecelia's companion wore a sleeveless flashy cotton dress. She was of medium height, at least as best I could tell, and she appeared more slender than she actually was. She had hair as black as midnight, but shorter than Cecelia's. She had a pointed chin and perfectly smooth, dark caramel skin. Of all her features, only the roan brown eyes were large; her forehead, mouth, and teeth were remarkably small. But the eyes told the story of a life consisting of too many lies. She offered me her hand. I noticed her fingernails were bitten down to the quick.

I shook it quickly, said hello and speaking to them both stated, "It's much more enjoyable to spend such a beautiful day with two attractive companions." They both smiled broad smiles back at me.

"I hope you don't mind?" I smiled with boyish charm.

"Not at all," Cecelia replied. "In fact, since you're such a baseball expert, maybe you can explain the game to us."

Smiling, I said, "Maybe later." I thought it best for the three of us just to enjoy the game before I told her about Lesley, since it wasn't the type of news one wanted to receive in a crowd. So I held up my left arm and yelled to the hot dog barker for three hot dogs with mustard for her, myself and her young friend. I was well aware that it constituted an indulgence of one of the seven deadly sins of the ballpark to put ketchup on a dog.

They each took a dog and slowly worked on them as we watched the Exporters and Indians struggle for a win to capture the lead of the Texas League. The most exciting part of the game was a fist-fight in the second inning between Beaumont's first basemen Rudy York and the Indian's pitcher

George Murray. When Rudy marched out to the mound, threw down his glove and the two huskies went to war. York won five-minute rhubarb, bringing crimson from Murray's nose and mouth with a powerhouse right that started from the left field bleachers.

The game finally ended in semi-darkness after more than three hours of hectic warfare. I noted that The Toad had gone 0 for 5 at the plate this afternoon. I quietly hoped that his wife's current problem hadn't edged its way into his life to such an extent that his game was now sliding into the tank.

When the fans slowly filtered down from the bleachers and out to their cars. I took Cecelia's hand and helped her out of the stands. With her friend walking several feet behind us, she looped her arm into mine like it belonged there. I enjoyed her touch. We continued on towards her car as I spoke calmly.

"If you have a few minutes, there's something I need to tell you."

She said okay and told her friend to wait by the car. We both stood there looking out into the field as the early evening star started its climb from over the main stadium bleachers behind home plate. When only the grounds crew and the cleaning crew remained in the stadium, I led Cecelia by the hand back to the first row of bleachers and sat on the first row with our feet kicking in the red dirt. "Cecelia, I've got something to tell you and I don't think you'll like to hear it much."

"Like my mother always told me when I was a child, if you got bad news, it's always best to come right out with it. So it's best, Mr. Nayland, that you just come out with it."

"Lesley Timons is dead and the sheriff's office is investigating it as a homicide."

She inhaled deeply and I could see her pulse quicken in her neck. The news struck her hard. She opened her small clutch purse and pulled an embroidered, white handkerchief and used it to wipe away the tears from the inside of her eyes and asked me.

"Do they know how it happened?" Cecelia said simply.

"Yes. He was shot once in the chest, possibly by someone he knew due to the fact it appeared the gun was discharged close up."

I thought it best not to mention that it was pretty clear he had been tied up like a steer before the final blow came.

She looked back up into my eyes, and her expression changed as quickly as a lightning strike. "Did that white whore do it?"

With as much professionalism as I could muster at that moment, and with her barely holding herself together, I stated a witness stand statement. "It doesn't appear so. From what I gathered from the evidence collected by sheriff investigators handling the case, it appears it was done by a fairly strong man."

With the assertiveness of a boot camp cadet, she stood quickly while placing her handkerchief back into her clutch bag.

"Thank you for sharing the game with me and my friend and the hot dogs, Mr. Nayland. And also for taking the time to tell me about what happen to Lesley."

Before I could offer to walk her to her car, she walked away briskly to catch up with her friend. I hoped she really had taken the news as well as she had just let on, but something told me this wouldn't be the last time I saw Cecelia regarding this case.

I decided to go have a chat with Niefhoff before he left the ball park. I headed around the outside of the park to the far left-field entrance which remained open after games to allow the ball-players a way out of the gates.

As I approached, six Indian ball players came out of the yard carrying gear bags heading to their cars. Two of which were the same two I'd danced with previously. I proceeded in behind them and walked over to the stairs that lead to the locker rooms. As I did so I noticed The Toad sitting on a bench against outfield fence cleaning his cleats with a Case pocket knife. I turned, went over, and stuck out my hand.

"Hi, my name's Lou. I've been watching you this season."

I sat next to him and continued in my best club-house dialect. "You know it appears to me you may be moving up next season with the way you handle the wood this summer."

He quit cleaning his cleats and looked at me with a dispassionate stare. "I reckon it's possible, but not with my golden sombrero at the plate today." He hesitated for a long southern moment. "I've had lots on my mind this week, family stuff. The guys tell me they suspect those problems will disappear as quickly as they appeared and that the wind was blowing favorable in my direction now and I should keep my dobber up."

I didn't react to that little insight and smiled back at him. "We've all had days like yours today."

"You played?" he asked with slight surprise.

I tipped my hat and nodded. "Yeah, back in the late teens, but I never made it out of the Texas League. Goofed my shoulder."

He looked at me with more interest now. "How'd did you shake them?"

I smiled a toothy grin. "You remind yourself it's just a day, and it's a long summer. One bad day doesn't mean you go making it worse by trying to correct your swing. Just bury the day and kept doing what your body knows is working."

He smiled. "Yeah, I reckon you're right."

I tried to help him keep his chin up and told him, "I've watched you most of this summer. You possess a strong, clean swing, so just relax in the box for the next game, don't think and let your body do what it knows how to do. It's really a simple game," I confessed. "Don't over-think it. You'll be fine."

He stood up. Put his cleats into his traveling bag, attempted a smile and said, "Thanks, Lou. It was nice to meet you." Nodding my way, he swung his bag over his shoulder and left the stadium.

As he walked out, I saw Bert coming up the locker room stairs.

I walked towards him. "Evening, Coach."

"Hey Lou, what you doing down here tonight?"

"I caught the game and thought I would see how things were progressing in your pennant run."

He kept walking out as he said, "It's looking good. Let's walk and talk, it's getting late and I would like to get home."

He continued talking, "The boys are looking better than I expected, actually. We're still in the league hunt. I thought they looked especially strong today, even though it ended horse to horse in the end. I think we will pull ahead with our home stand next week when we return."

"You get my vote for Coach of the Year," I replied.

We walked a distance in silence before he spoke again. "You solve that society dame's case you asked me about last week?"

"No," I replied, not wanting to tell him about the Timons kid's death or how it might be was connected to the Camp's. So I asked him about Johnny instead.

"How's the Toad been playing this week?"

He stopped at his car and threw his gear bag into the back seat and turned to look straight at me. "He's had a good two weeks, batting close to .290. No errors in the field. Tonight's performance being out of the norm for him, but I'm sure he'll be back on track Monday."

I smiled at him while still attempting to dig a little. "So you've heard nothing more in the dugout that would concern you with regards to our conversation?"

He shook his head as he spoke. "Nope, nothing. Like I said, his game has been good."

"Glad to hear it," I responded.

"There have been some clues that may mean the problem may have solved itself recently. I'll let you know as soon as I confirm some details."

He thanked me and I wished him good luck as he closed his door. I headed back to my car.

I walked wearily down Fourth, rounded the corner onto Virginia Avenue. A full moon shone in the sky, enlarged and blurred by wispy clouds. Its light fell on the ballpark fence, casting eerie shadows onto the street. I was struck by the beauty and peace of the night.

The serenity was soon broken when a large dark figure stepped away from the shadows of the outfield fence and spoke calmly.

"Evening, Shamus. Enjoy the game today?"

I turned to see the Jersey kid walking towards me. He stopped a dozen feet away, set his canvas gear bag down, withdrew his ash Louisville Slugger from within and twirled the bat in his right hand in complete circles.

"Actually, I did," I responded as I swung the driver side door open to form a wall between us. I was relieved to see he wasn't accompanied by the big Swede tonight.

"You're not still digging into the Camp couple's private life?"

I slowly reached in and grasped the police night stick I keep lodged beside the driver's seat without letting the kid see it. "Not in any way that concerns you," I replied

The kid stepped forward. "I thought we made it clear that you were to leave Johnny and Lauren alone." He stated as he swung his personal piece of lumber, smacking the sweet spot of the barrel in the palm of his left hand.

"Oh, I got your message, but I'm a slow learner. And, besides, I'm on their side, not against it."

I needed to get out without this turning physical. One, I didn't want to hurt the Indians' chances in the pennant race. Two, I figured this kid was just a knot-head sticking up for a teammate or a guardian angel sent by old man Davis to keep the kid clear of mischief. He certainly wasn't a blackmailing mastermind. So with that in mind, I spoke calmly and let go of the night stick behind the car door and held both my hands up, palms out. "Whoa, big hitter, I'm not here to make trouble, just watching a game and talking to the girls."

He smirked. "All right. So maybe you won't get any trouble from me tonight."

I had a feeling his heart wasn't really in it to crush my skull. He was just playing out his part. But he continued speaking. "Besides, gumshoe, I heard on the street that one of the concerned parties wasn't hanging around town anymore." He went on, spreading oil, "He's had a higher calling, as they say... so I guess your services won't be needed even if you are on the Camp's team."

I kept my hands up as he kept his eyes on me while he put his bat back into the canvas bag and slung it over his shoulder. He started to walk away but yelled back, "You stay just a fan, Shamus, or else." He grinned, turned and yelled over his shoulder, "Abyssinia, gumshoe." He finished in his distinctive Jersey accent.

I watched him walk away as I sat in my Ford, slightly shaken. I let the tumblers in my head determine what part, if any, Jersey Boy played in this current drama other than henchman for Davis. I wasn't going to answer that question sitting in my car, and I had no place else to dig in the dark. So I headed back to my apartment to prepare myself for the dreaded call to Mrs. Camp in the morning.

Chapter Twenty-Four

I'd a long and pleasantly intoxicating Saturday night at Irene's and a fitful Sunday night, I slowly crawled out of bed early Monday morning, switched on the radio and tuned it to 1520 for the morning weather report. I plodded into the kitchen to make a fresh pot of Joe. The radio announcer, with a twangy voice, predicted it would be another burner with temps maxing out the mercury by noon with little or no breeze. A cold shower seemed to be the ideal way to get this day going.

The more I thought on the different angles in the case, the more I became convinced that the bleeding someone was attempting to put on the Camp dame was personally motivated and not a money grab. This was my brilliant conclusion as I sat sipping my coffee, waiting for the toaster to pop.

Having delayed as long as possible calling Lauren to give her the details of Timons' death and after pouring myself a second cup of Joe, I dialed her number, 7-0515, knowing The Toad wouldn't likely answer the phone because the Indians were traveling to Texas this week. I had my story ready: the plain truth, with a little varnish on the rough spots. "Damn, busy signal."

I returned to the kitchen, freshened my cup. Dawdled back to my nightstand, grabbed my leather-bound notepad and made my way back into the living room to the phone, sat on the couch while putting the phone into my lap and dialed again. The phone rang a half-dozen times before I heard someone pick up the receiver and, in a weeping, whispering voice, say, "Hello?"

"Lauren, this is Lou, you all right?"

I could guess she was wiping her tears away with a handkerchief as she

158

spoke. "Yes, excuse me, I'm just a tad off this morning." Her speech was small and thin and her words shimmered as she asked, "Is there something I can help you with, Mr. Nayland?"

Her voice sounded sad, and what I had to tell her wouldn't make her feel any better. "I was just calling to check on you this morning and see if you had heard about the unfortunate events of Friday night?"

"Yes, Mr. Nayland, I read about the passing of an acquaintance of mine yesterday morning in the Sunday paper. It's very sad." There wasn't a half-tone, a shading, in voice or manner, to indicate that she was talking about anything half as serious as murder.

She continued as if she might be talking about the weather. "I need to tell you something that is for your ears only. You see, I saw Lesley at my place the night before they found his body."

I paused briefly. "I appreciate your confidence and I will protect your secret the best I can." I sat silently with the receiver to my ear before I asked, "Is there anything I can do for you today?"

"No, I'll be fine. Thanks for asking though."

I decided to push her a little. "Do you believe that your friend's passing will resolve the issues you came to see me about?"

She paused for what seemed like ten minutes. "No, Mr. Nayland, I don't believe my problems have gone away. And to be honest, as I read through the news this morning, I've come to the conclusion that Lesley's death is just the beginning of my worst fears of my secret coming out." She hesitated before she asked, "Can I assume that Mr. Timon's accident was your way of solving my issues?"

I let the question hang in the air.

The long silence seemed to unnerve her, but then with a questioning air and regained strength in her voice she asked, "Was it?"

I understood why she may have asked the question, but it didn't mean I liked the assertion.

"No, Mrs. Camp, killing isn't a method I use to solve my clients' problems, no matter what amount of money they may pay. I would have thought you would know that about me before you hired me."

"Yes, of course, Mr. Nayland, I had to ask, but I've heard you can be hard, very hard."

"I understand it's a difficult morning for you, so I will just let that pass," I replied. "I assume you want me to continue on the case to uncover your letter writer?"

"Yes! You must! I want you to get whoever is doing this. You appear to be good and kind, but I've learned that at times you're mean and cruel, vicious even. I'm appealing to that mean streak in you, your nasty side, get whoever is doing this. So he'll never be able to hurt another." I heard her take a deep breath and exhale before continuing. "Like I said, I feel this second note is just the beginning of my difficulties, not a sign of a conclusion." She spoke the final words under total control and with a brisk firmness.

"All right, I'll do the best I can," I told her. "I'll call you tomorrow after I check out another lead I'm developing."

She thanked me. We both hung up at the same time.

After I got off the horn, I was certain I should make a little run down to Norman tomorrow morning to have an indirect conversation with her older brother, Brock. There was something about his general demeanor and his interest in Sister Aimee McPherson during our brief meeting that had been nagging in the recesses of my mind ever since. Even if my suspicions about him were wrong, he may still be helpful in providing a name or names that might point me in the right direction. I figured I could resurrect my disguise as a baseball scout and casually drop by his office on my way into the University baseball complex.

The phone rang. "Hello."

"Lou, its Flatten. Can you meet me this evening? I've a couple of things I need to tell you."

"Sure, where and when do you want to meet?"

"Meet me at the New Empire Club around eight o'clock."

"Okay, I'll be in the Press Club upstairs. Come on up and we'll talk."

Since I now had a plan for tonight and tomorrow, I figured the most productive use of my afternoon should be used to check in with Coach Neihoff. I had run into the Jersey Boy too often in this case and hadn't yet figured out the totality of his part in this little drama. I hoped Bert might be talkative on the subject since he would be just supervising the Indians' batting practice this afternoon. I slipped on my shoes, grabbed my jacket and headed out the door.

Chapter Twenty-Five

I walked down the front of Holland Field to the turnstiles and slipped in under the front bleachers. I hadn't walked ten steps when Putter appeared like a ghost at my side.

"Afternoon, Mr. Nayland."

"Hi, Putter, Coach around?"

"Yeah, he's sitting in the dugout watching batting practice."

Before I could follow up with another question, we both noticed the local sportswriter, Ross Vass, walking toward us from the third baseline entrance. As he got closer, I noticed that he was slightly cross-eyed behind his gold wire-rim glasses. Putter must have noticed it at the same time because we both gave each other a queered look.

Vass recognized me almost simultaneously and with a huge grin asked, "Lou Nayland, what the hell are you doing at the ballpark at this time of day?"

I grinned sardonically back at him. "Just a fan watching a little hitting practice."

He took a pencil from his hat-band like he was conducting an interview.

"When guys in your line of work show up someplace it usually means trouble for someone. Got anything you care to share?" he asked as he pulled a writing pad out of his right suit pocket.

"Sorry, Mack, but I'm just here to watch the batting and figure the odds on the team's chances for the pennant."

Vass shrugged his shoulders, tipped his hat at us and headed toward the exit.

As soon as he was out of sight I grabbed off my hat and spat in it. It was a fairly new hat, too. "What's the matter with you, Nayland?" Putter asked, surprised.

I looked at him sternly. "Spit in your hat quick," I answered, not thinking for a minute he'd follow my directions.

"What's the idea?" he asked as he replaced his ball cap.

I cheerfully told him, "The worst possible jinx in the world is to see a crossed-eyed man inside your ballpark," I replied. "And I hate to be responsible for the Indians being jinxed out of the pennant when it was within my power to prevent such an event."

"I've seen many a jinx do all kinds nasty things to a professional ballplayer. I have seen one make a .300 hitter faultier and start batting like Grasshopper Lillie and then there was a great pitcher who become a bad one in a week. I've heard of whole ball clubs, composed of educated men, carry a dead rooster with them on every away game because the catcher's jealous wife came from a family of gypsies who put a hex on them. So their captain went to see another gypsy who told him the only way to stave off the jinx was to carry around the dead rooster."

He was interested, so I continued. "Luck is a combination of confidence and getting the breaks. If the dead rooster makes you lucky, then it does, because you have confidence."

Putter nodded in agreement as he proceeded to cross-examine my knowledge in this area further. "But what about all those ball-players who masticate the weed?" he asked. "Do they kill jinxes, too?"

I admitted to him that they were the main exterminators of the jinx.

He beamed as he tilted his ball cap up. "I'm glad that the percentage of wearers of cross-eyes is small." He turned and walked away, chuckling. I walked to the end of the bleachers onto the field behind third base.

The smell of freshly cut summer grass filled my nose. It brought back a flood of memories of my adolescence and playing ball. Smell truly is the only one of our senses that can fill our minds with such vivid images of our youth. As I took it in, I knew it was one shared by all athletics that spent any time on the grass because in those brief moments of recollection, we each, all, become young again.

I continued over to where Bert was sitting in the dugout.

He looked up as I approached. "Hi, Lou." He snubbed out his cigarette on the bench as he rose and shook my outstretched hand.

He sat down and pointed to the empty space beside him.

"What brings you down here today?" he asked.

I took out a cigarette, offered him one, which he politely took. I noticed again how clear and bright the coach's eyes were. I knew there was an even keener mind behind them. To the outsider looking in that dugout that day, Coach might appear to be a sluggish old burnout of a manager dozing on the bench. But his eyes told me different. He saw every throw of the ball and every swing of the bat from each kid playing before him in the hot haze of the afternoon.

I took a drag and watched the next batter step into the box to bat and answered, "Not much."

"Mostly I wanted some fresh air and a chance to come down and remind myself of my youth."

He grinned. "It gets harder every year to get there, doesn't it?"

His team's current lead in the pennant race must have had him in a good mood because he quietly sang a little ditty:

"*Oh, the days of the Kerry dancing,*
Oh, the ring of the piper's tune,
Oh, for one of those hours of gladness,
Gone, alas, like our youth, too soon...."

As he trailed off, I watched as the Toad stepped into the batter's box and let two curve balls blow by him. On the third pitch, a high hanging fast ball, he made perfect contact on the sweet spot and sent that ball on a ride over the right field fence.

I turned to Bert. "He just might be the next Buzz Arlett." I smiled.

Bert shrugged his shoulders maybe, while he kept looking as his feet as he used his cleats to scratch the caked red dirt off the sides of each of his shoes as he reflected on baseball. So I took another drag and waited for his wit and wisdom.

He slowly looked up into the blue sky and spoke in a low tone. "For me, the game has become different from my day when I started back in 1913 from what it is today. I don't mean just that the fences were further back, and the ball was deader and all the other changes." Slightly smiling, he ran on. "I mean, it was more fun to play ball then. The players were more colorful, you know, because we drew them from every stratus of life, and the whole sport was kind of topsy-turvy most of the time, not the highly organized business in every detail it has become today."

I let him talked. Figuring it was the best way to get to my questions.

"All of it was pretty exciting for a young kid, but I wasn't a young kid by the time I got to the show, I was close to thirty, but I'd never been anywhere before baseball so I enjoyed it all."

He took several puffs off his cigarette as he reflected and then continued. "In my day baseball attracted all sorts of people. You had tough guys, mild guys, stupid guys, crazy guys, college-educated men, city slickers, and hayseeds from the country. And back then country kids were really country kids, real rubes. Nowadays I don't see much difference between city slickers and country kids, at least not like they used to be."

As he sat in silence, I thought his last line was as good as any place to insert my questions about his Jersey Boy. "What do you know about your boy from Jersey?"

He snapped back from reflection and became serious. "Why do you ask?"

"To be honest, Coach, I've bumped into him a few times away from the field and in settings he doesn't seem natural in."

His eyes became cold gray, and he looked me straight in the eyes with more seriousness than I believed he possessed. "My advice to you is to give the kid a wide berth if at all possible." The way he spoke the line unnerved me.

Then he asked, "Does he have something to do with the Toad case?"

I shook my head. "I'm not sure yet, but he has some interest in the kid. I'm just not sure if it's being a teammate protecting a country kid or there's something else behind it."

"Either way, Lou, give him a wide berth!"

"Really, can I ask why, Coach?"

He looked around to make sure no one was near us. "Your Jersey Boy, as you call him, is from Newark. He doesn't play under his actual name. His real name is Antonio Amoria. His mother is a sister to New Jersey crime boss Stefano Badami of the Elizabeth Crime family. His father is Flippo Amoria, Stefano's under boss. From what I've gathered, his mother encouraged his interest in baseball to keep him from being involved in the Castellammarese War. She succeeded as far as I can tell. We had him checked out when he signed with the club. He's never been arrested or been in any serious trouble, but he did grow up in poor Italian neighborhood in Jersey, around some ruthless relatives, so my bet is he knows how to fight and possibly kill."

"I wouldn't want to get on his bad side nor test his seriousness in either skill. Besides, he's a great infielder and fair at the plate, and I've had no problems with him. So he's Jake in my book."

I snubbed out the butt of the cigarette burning between my fingers. I hadn't realized I had stopped smoking it during his speech. I stood up and watch the next batter step into the box for practice. "I have a thought Coach and I would like your opinion."

I turned and faced him. "Do you think The Toad's father-in-law would hire the Jersey Boy to keep an eye on his son-in-law and out of trouble, or would Antonio be working something for the family back home? Odds?"

"If I were to guess, Lou, I would say he's working for the father-in-law and not the family. If you want odds, I would say its three to one the kids straight and just looking after The Toad."

"So you could say your both working for the same side, but I would still remain cautious around him."

"Well, I'll assume you're correct on your analysis. You know these boys better than most." Then I grinned back. "But I'll also be cautious."

I looked out onto the field at the youngster throwing pitches at The Toad and stated, "Your new hurler seems to have a good arm."

Bert laughed, "It's the same every year. The rituals of the game never vary."

"These kids all think there the reincarnation of Walter Johnson. When in fact they have nothing more on the ball than the autograph of the league president."

"Hell Lou, you know as well as I do that for ninety percent of these kids in the minors it's all a fantasy land. Some agent convinces them they're going to be the next Ruth and sells the same to some ball club as they mumble off hand during the contract signing, if he ever learns to hit." We both laughed out loud.

He stood up, and we shook hands as he headed out to the mound to talk to his young pitchers, throwing batting practice. I walked out onto the field, took another smell of the cut grass and headed to my car.

Chapter Twenty-Six

It was 8:00 p.m., breakfast time in a casino, as I walked down the side stairs of a run-down building on Reno into the New Empire rooms located in the basement. The New Empire was one of the few upscale gambling clubs to be found in the city. It was owned either directly or indirectly by a local shyster by the name of Oban Chester Patterson, the undisputed King of the Underworld. Since the teens Patterson with the aid of his Democratic political friends held a virtual monopoly in bootlegging, gambling, prostitution and narcotics. He collected his percentages in the form of monthly retainers for legal services from his operators.

The swells of the city liked the New Empire and made it successful because they came for the good food, mostly honest games, beautiful women, and a good drink on the side.

I headed toward the stairs for the Press Club upstairs. The platoons of slots were getting a steady play, and their whirr-clunk, thunk-clatter dominated the sounds of the big room. There's a 1 in a 2400 chance of hitting the jackpot, and those odds remained the same on the first pull as well as the last. Real gamblers never played them. They were installed mostly to entertain the wives of the real gamblers who played the games of chance with better odds. The best for these guys were, of course, the craps tables where the house held only a two percentage advantage over the rollers.

Under the sounds of the slots you could make out the chant of the croupiers as I stopped near the craps pit. I nodded to the stick-man, a guy called Swift Tony. Every house-run crap game in the world has a stickman, and just about every stick-man uses a curved stick to return the dice to the shooter.

I'd known Tony ever since I got him out of scrap involving a bad marriage with a grifter.

Anyone one with common sense knew Patterson didn't make his money by having dishy dames in bright costumes and black mesh stockings shagging drinks to the patrons, but from the house percentages from the tables. And if luck turned in a gambler's favor, the house had guys like Tony to help keep the money in the house.

They way that usually works was a sucker would come in and start shooting. At the start of his roll he got a whole basket of Tony's dice, every one of them honest to pick from. Any two dice in the basket he liked, those were the dice he used. Well, as long as he kept shooting for reasonable stakes, he'd keep those dice. Every time he'd shoot, Tony slide the dice back to him with his stick, and he'd roll them out again. The house would take its percentage out of the side bets, the roller would win-a-little-lose-a-little, and everybody would be happy, particularly Tony and the house.

That's the way things usually go at any crap table. The bets fairly even, no arguments, honest dice, pass, miss, pass, and the percentage gradually dragging all the money out of everybody's pockets.

But there are emergencies that do come up now and then. Some guy will get hot and start letting his bets ride, which means he doubles his money with every pass he makes. When someone starts doing that, that's when Tony's well-crafted skills with his stick come into play.

He lets the shooter use the perfectly honest dice on his next throw. If it comes out right there on one roll, if he rolls seven or eleven, that is, he's a winner and the house hopes he rolls again. He may crap out on that roll, too; that is, he may hit two, three, or twelve, and lose right there, but most likely he'll catch a point; that is, he'll roll four, five, six, eight, nine, or ten. And then he's got to make his point, roll that number again before he rolls a seven, and the percentage's say he's not likely to do that. That's why even honest crap table will make money. But percentage doesn't say he can't or he won't do it, just that he's not likely to do it.

That's where Tony comes in with his stick and sleight of hand to switch out the roller's dice for two loaded ones to ensure he doesn't leave the place with his winnings.

I looked upon what appeared to be an honest game being run tonight by Tony, tipped my hat, turned and climbed the stairs to the second floor.

Stepping onto the lush carpet of the Press Club, I looked around to see if Flatten had arrived yet. The room contained a small bar and a dozen tables with upholstered chairs around each. Unlike down below, the room didn't have a slot machine or any kind of gambling. The Press Club was a private operation run by oilmen, politicians and newspapermen for themselves and a few others who were willing to pay a certain amount a year for the privilege. My dues were paid by a former client who said my fee wasn't enough for what I'd done for him.

Flatten hadn't arrived, so I went to a corner booth, sat and waited for Flatten to show up. A large man of color dressed in a white shirt and red vest came over. "Scotch and water, neat please," I said.

When he departed I noticed Flatten emerge on the top of the stairs. I motioned to the security man that he was okay. So he let him pass, allowing him to come over and have a seat at my table.

"Your scotch and water, sir," the waiter stated before asking, "Is your guest going to have a drink as well?"

Flatten said, "Just a beer, please."

When the waiter left, he slid his chair closer. "After you left the other day, I made some inquiries, especially after I heard about the murder of the colored musician that occurred over the weekend."

"And?" I asked.

"First, from what I've gathered, I don't think his demise was the result of any activity involving the secret society you asked about. Second, it's rumored that someone was blackmailing him or someone close to him in connection to him running around with some white broad down in the Deuce, but the police haven't learned about that detail as of yet."

The waiter returned with the beer and then quickly stepped back to the bar.

When he departed, Flatten resumed with his report. "Finally, the word on the street is that the blackmailer isn't anyone from the colored community, because almost everyone down there already knew about his dalliances. Most the coloreds say that dirty politics is behind it in an attempt to hold sway over high-ranking politicians, because the white gal Timons ran around with is one of their daughters."

We drank in silence as I reflected on what he'd told me.

"So you're sure the Klan angle is out in the murder and the blackmailing scheme." I asked.

"Best I can tell, yes, and for the record I wouldn't put much weight on the politician's daughter angle. It's likely just bigoted bias from the Deuce crowd."

I dug into my pocket, took out a ten spot and slid it across the table and under his beer. "Can you do me one more thing, quietly asked around and find out the names of any friends of the deceased musician who might know anything about who was blackmailing him."

"Thanks," Flatten said as he picked up his beer. "I'll let you know if I hear anything."

I finished my drink and walked past Tony on my way out. The table appeared cold now that Flatten was tossing the dice. I exited the club and went home for the night.

Chapter Twenty-Seven

A freak early fall-like rain occurred during the night. The air, now cooler, possessed the colored freshness of a butterfly emerging from his chrysalis. I walked to my window and took in a large breath of the cool morning breeze. I hoped this unusual weather marked a change in my investigation into Mrs. Camp's blackmailing.

I put on a pot of coffee and jumped into a cold shower to shake off the edges of sleepiness still fogging my brain. After drinking two cups of Joe, I walked down the back stairs of the apartment, and greeted Mrs. Giannasi toting her vacuum up. "Hello, ma'am." I continued down to my car in the parking lot as I yelled back at her, "I expect to look into your sister's problem later this week."

"Blessa you'ah, dear, and gratcie."

I walked out the rear door. A mockingbird erupted from a red-berried bush near the rear of my car, sailed up to the gutter and yelled curses at me. A large, yellow tabby sprinted out from under my car, settled on the back steps, and gave me a smirk only cats possess. I shrugged, settled in behind the wheel and started up the V-6.

I drove through midtown, past the Warner Theater. The marquee's white bulbs flickered on and off with Errol Flynn in *Captain Blood* in large black letters blazed in its center and in smaller letters *Night at the Opera*, with the Marx Brothers, as the matinee showing.

I accelerated east to catch U.S. 77 on the eastside of downtown. Apart from a few trucks, there was no traffic. I smoothly turned onto the highway and exceeded the posted speed limit by ten mph as I continued south to

Norman and parked in front of the campus.

I walked by the flowering shrubbery running along the path under the red and white stone brick archway that led onto the main north oval campus. I tried to do a bit of thinking while I hiked by a row of blooming rose bushes towards the three-storied Holmberg Hall. But a guy has to have a few additional facts to build his guesses on. The hall's architecture represented the "Cherokee Gothic" movement of the southwest, with twin towers that crawled towards the clear blue sky. It just resembled a government building to me.

I stopped two giggling co-eds who wore calf length crimson cotton skirts and starched white blouses as they walked out the doors of Holmberg Hall. "Excuse me, could you tell me where Professor Camp's office is?"

The tall, fresh faced, blonde with sun freckles giggled and said, "He's on the third floor at the south end of the hall." She smiled at her plump, shorter, redheaded friend as they strolled out onto the green in front of the main administration building towards a large group of kids sitting under one of the dominant oak trees in the middle of the north quad.

I entered, and the stairs were to my right, uneven and worn from the thousands of young feet that had coursed up and down them since the school's creation in 1918. The stairs ended on the third floor. I marched along the marbled trimmed corridor examining each brass name plate screwed to the smoked glass doors in my search for Professor Camp's office.

Toward the end of the hall, I noticed one of the doors slightly ajar. The brass plate read *Associate Professor Brock Camp*. I knocked with the respect of a stranger in a strange land.

His clear tenor voice said, "Come in."

"Sorry to bother you, Professor Camp, but I thought I should at least say hello as I was on campus today scouting some student ball players."

He looked at me suspiciously, but proceeded with an unnatural calmness. "I'm happy you did. It's always nice to receive friends of the family in my humble surroundings."

"I hope you're not too busy," I said as I walked into his small office.

"You must lead a very interesting life, Mr. Nayland."

"I enjoy it," I replied.

He spoke casually as I examined the books lining his shelves. "I mean with all the traveling you do to ascertain talents of all those young men?"

I continued to browse his papers and books with an apparently casual eye. "It is, and I enjoy the opportunity to help these young men get started in a career that I love so dearly."

He leaned back in his office chair as he interlocked his fingers, palms down, onto his chest. "Then you enjoy the work you do and the places you go?"

I stopped in front of his small white oak desk and sat in the slate backed chair used by the students. "I would say I'm very lucky to have the opportunity to do what I do."

"You see, I love the game. I played a season as a professional when I was much younger, and I still haven't lost my love of the game or my minor involvement in its process."

He listened but appeared uninterested. "Then I would say you're a very lucky man indeed, Mr. Nayland."

He smiled a non-committal smile as he continued. "I, myself, have struggled a long time to find contentment in my career or place in this universe."

I listen to him pontificate on career choices, when I inadvertently noticed the book, *Titus Andronicus*, the same torn little paperback he had been reading that day at his grandmother's. The well dog-eared copy was now lying on the corner of his desk.

I looked back his way. "Have you found joy in your work here as a professor?"

He sat forward. "I would have to say that teaching fills the coffers of my personal earthly needs, but not my spiritual needs. You see, Mr. Nayland, I believe one's accomplishments in life aren't just tied to one's financial success but rather to the individual's ability to affect the circumstances of his fellow man."

He now had my attention. "Is that an important aspect in your life, Professor?"

Excitedly he responded, "Very much so, yes. But until quite recently I haven't been able to fulfill that particular need."

I sat in the chair, rubbing a knuckled behind my ear lobe considering everything he said or may be intimating. "Then am I to take it you have recently discovered a solution to that requirement in your life?"

He stood quickly and walked with his hands clasped at his back to the lone window in his office.

"Yes, I have," he stated with too much enthusiasm and for the first time some feeling showed on his face. "Sister Aimee has shown me the light and granted divine guidance upon me to do the things that are required to remove the moral decay of this great nation and to bring about the betterment of mankind."

Our conversation drifting into divine guidance made me uncomfortable. I could now see where a disciple of Sister Aimee might consider Lauren's love of jazz, and everything that entailed as a detriment to the morals of American society. The professor's elation with his newly found purpose in life made me uneasy. I needed to probe further to determine if he was aware of his sister's current circumstances.

He seemed talkative, so I encouraged him further. "Can I ask you what you believe you must do to fill this spiritual void?"

He turned and there seemed to be tears forming at the edges of his eyes as he spoke. "Our nation has drifted from its founding faith, allowing its people to become immoral and sinful. But, Sister Aimee has revealed that people, like me, must stand up to these backsliders and provide them guidance through any means at our disposal."

It suddenly dawned on me that his beliefs sounded eerily similar to the threats made in his sister's letters. But many people in the South had similar beliefs. It didn't mean he, or others connected to Sister Aimee, were the blackmailer or, worse, a murderer. But his words and thoughts on morality still concerned me. They could very well be the type of motives that resulted in blackmail. I thought best to let him preach on rather than cross-exam him at this point.

Suddenly, his temperament changed as quickly as the weather does in Oklahoma in May. Rapid temperament changes appeared to be something he and his sister shared in common.

"I'm sorry, Mr. Nayland, for my excited outburst. It's usually not in my nature to lose my composure. But I have found such inspiration from Sister Aimee. The Spirit has been moving me in exciting directions."

He walked back behind his desk and sat down. "I'm sure I'm taking up too much of your time when you should be elsewhere taking care of your own business." He flicked his hand in my direction as he began to read something on his desk.

"Thank you for stopping in, Mr. Nayland, and good luck with your pursuits on campus today." Clearly, I was being dismissed.

I was silent for a moment, thinking that Brock's statements were too glib, too pat. While everything he said more or less checked with the events that had developed, none of it really jibed. But at this point I had nothing, so I stood up and told him, "Thanks for your time, Professor, I'm sure we'll see each other again."

He nodded in my direction without taking his eyes off the papers when I walked out of his office and down the hall.

The dull gears in my brain slowly turned as I attempted to process what had just happened in the professor's office. The process was being slowed by the continuing, nagging thoughts I still had regarding how Timons had met his maker. I couldn't quite shake the feeling that the book the professor had been reading at the house and now lying on the corner of his desk were somehow connected to this whole mystery. I knew the details of Timons' demise faintly reminded me of a death in literature. I guessed it had been something I had read in Mrs. Fabor's English class back at El Dorado Junior College twenty years ago. I walked out of Holmberg Hall, feeling for the first time as though I was getting someplace on this bizarre case as I crossed the north oval, past the Administration building, towards the library in hopes I could find further clues, or a well-read and helpful librarian.

Chapter Twenty-Eight

I entered the library and headed straight to the reference desk where a young co-ed with curly hair the color of pine shavings in a sleeveless white sweater and crimson skirt filing index cards into a small receptacle of the card catalogue. Her sun-kissed shoulders brought a smile to my face.

As I stopped in front of her she swayed towards me, wafting in flowery odors from the slopes of her young body and asked, "May I help you with something?"

I smiled. "Could you, or someone, help me with books on English literature or possible a book of plays that include murder as a main plot line?"

She looked at me with a slight suspicion, as if surprised someone like me would be inquiring about a book. Hiding her thoughts she said, "I doubt I would be of much help to you, it's not my area of study."

She was a sweet, and I was curious, so I asked, "What is your area of study, may I ask?"

"I'm a junior in medical studies," she said with pride.

"What?" I said. "Huh?"

She laughed. "Everybody looks that way when I say I'm studying medicine." She hesitated. "But I won't be for much longer if I don't raise more tuition money, that's why I'm working in the library this term."

"Well, I hope it all works out, I bet you would be a great," I said with encouragement.

"Thank you," she said. "I believe our research librarian, Miss Swalia, could help you in what you're looking for. She's our resident expert on Shakespeare and English literature."

She turned to a bespectacled redheaded woman, who upon first glance appeared to be a typical middle-aged librarian sitting behind a large oak desk in a well-lit alcove. "Miss Swalia, could you help this gentleman?"

When she stood up and approached the young co-ed and I, it quickly became apparent the lady was closer to thirty than fifty. With hair color like a brush fire at night, a pleasant plump face, and dimpled pink cheeks with small sun freckles that ran across the bridge of her nose. She wore a lavender-flowered white summer dress that if the state highway commission built roads with that many curves, every driver in Oklahoma would need sea sick pills. With one look I knew she was butter and eggs, especially if you have a weakest for redheads, and I do.

As the young co-ed asked the question she placed a pair of square framed tortoise-shell glasses upon her nose. Her eyes were green and inconsistent like the sea. They said, "what the hell" and the glasses hadn't hidden the fact this woman was definitely different from the usual twists I encountered. She had a look of intelligence that made most men nervous and uncomfortable. And yet, she possessed the presence that I found most alluring in a woman, whether she be a wife, a maid, or a widow.

She rose decisively but gracefully, as though she had practiced the movement in front of a mirror. I followed her youthful bosom and tight sheathed hips across the carpeted floor. I felt sorry for any man that warmed themselves at that secret electricity. I almost forgot Irene's name for a moment as she spoke.

"Can I help you?" she inquired.

I was like a teenage boy asking a girl to the Sadie Hawkins dance. I had it so bad I couldn't keep the befuddled grin off my face. But I attempted to gather myself and repeated what I'd asked the young co-ed reference clerk regarding English literature.

She removed her glasses and rested the tip of the ear-piece upon her chin. She was good. She was very good. The way she smiled, when her lips parted, as she asked in a half serious and half teasing tone, "Could you possibly be more specific? Mr....?"

I pointed to an open table and gestured that we should sit down.

After we both took a seat on the hard pine chairs, I extended a hand and introduced myself. "Hello, my name is Lou Nayland. And you are?"

She took my hand and shook it firmly. "Nancy Swalia, Mr. Nayland." Her odor was faint and fragrant, like nostalgia from half-forgotten summers. The clasp of her hand sent a thrill up my arm and through my body. I reproached myself for possessing, in my thirties, the sudden emotion of a teenager. I released her hand and hesitantly asked. "Miss Swalia, right?"

Adjusting her glasses further up her nose, she looked directly into my eyes and replied, "Yes."

With a goofy smile, I continued. "You see, I have a limited knowledge of literature and practically none in Shakespearean plays, but I'm aware that he could write a really good murder scene. I'm trying to find a play that contains specific criminal acts of such."

She looked directly at me with her gleaming green eyes and stated, "Unusual question. May I inquire why?"

"Absolutely," I sputtered quickly.

But before I could continue, she followed up with, "Are you a writer researching a book?"

I shook my head no. I was quickly getting the impression that only honesty was my best bet with this intelligent bird. "See, I'm a private detective on a case."

She slightly tilted her head to the left and a very subtle grin formed on her mouth. "That may be the most interesting thing a man has said to me all week. I've often thought that the life of a detective would be an intensely interesting one. You see, I rather fancy myself a student of human nature, and though my studies have been clearly academic, you might say. I find the stories of unusual men quit interesting." A broad smile crossed her lips with the declaration.

"I have no doubt you're a good student on the subject," I declared.

With a playful smile still on her lips, she asked, "Isn't it true that one sees deepest into human nature in moments of strain, moments of crisis? You know those kinds of moments that must be delectably frequent in your line of work, Mr. Nayland?"

I doubted I could compete with her mind, but I tried to. "You see deep enough into certain aspects of human nature, I guess. But to be honest, most of the things I've seen I'd just as soon as forget," I said with seriousness.

"Such as?" she asked as her eyes brightened with curiosity.

"Hatred."

"Greed."

"And jealousy, which has made many of men lose their sophistication," I said with a knowledgeable grin.

She remained silent, so I finished my thought. "Those are the three emotions that cause most passion crimes, and then there's the fourth, and maybe the worst, impersonal love of inflicting pain."

We both sat in the stillness of the library before I spoke. "I'll tell you what, Nancy. When we are both free on a sunny Saturday afternoon, I'll get a bottle of my favorite scotch and we can sit and discuss the evils of mankind until your heart's content. But today I really must get on with the details of my case." I reached over and touched her fingers spread across the desk and smiled.

She didn't take her hand off mine, but stated coyly, "Another time then, Lou."

We sat in silence of the moment before I asked, "Think you can help me?"

"It's kind of a non-specific inquiry. What else can you give me?"

Without being graphic, I gave her the general details of Timons' murder, as well as the title of the book Brock Camp had on his desk, *Titus Andronicus*.

Her eyes turn hard. "That is a nasty piece of literature and definitely the very definition of a Greek tragedy." Still holding my hand, she continued. "The play is set in Rome during Imperial times and tells the tale of General Titus and his cycle of revenge with Tamora, Queen of the Goths."

I nodded, so she went on.

"Most readers of his plays considered it to be Shakespeare's bloodiest and most violent work."

I smiled at her. "You know your stuff. Bloodiest, you say?"

"And it's extremely violent," she said as our eyes met and kindled an indissolvable bond of understanding.

The shared spell was broken as I pushed on with my questions. "Is the murder described in the play similar to the details I just gave you?"

Maintaining a scholarly demeanor, she said, "There are several murders described in the play. One gruesome death, in particular, is the death of Lavinia."

I sat in silence and let her explain. "The murder I recall centers around two men, Demetrius and Chiron, who have killed Lavinia's husband and then drag Lavinia into the woods to rape her. And after doing so, violently, they chop off her hands and cut out her tongue so she cannot reveal their identities. There are others that are killed in the play, but Lavinia's death fits the details you described to me in your case."

"I think you're right about the several similarities in Lavinia's death as you just described and the murder I'm investigating."

"You know what, Lou? I think the guy you're looking for is a pedagogue."

"A what?"

"A pedagogue, you know, a teacher."

Pleasant as our growing interplay was, we both knew this is where it ended today. Her last statement had hit me like a thunderbolt. I knew who the blackmailer was as we stood up and pushed in our chairs. I thanked and shook Miss Nancy Swalia's hand quickly. "You've been a great help, thanks!" She slowly released my hand as I gave her my card, and since I'm not Oscar Wilde, I resisted the temptation to grab her and plant a honey cooler upon her full lips.

We both turned and smiled to one another as I nearly sprinted back along the study tables towards the exit as I added as quietly as possible over my shoulder, "If there's anything you ever need, anything, just call that number day or night."

She replied with a slight laugh. "I might just do that, Mr. Nayland." She had a nice voice I still think of at times.

The parallels between Lavinia's and Timons's deaths along with Brock's monologue suddenly made sense. The strands of the case were now coming together like the themes of a complex piece of music, and the score now erased all doubts; Brock was both a killer and blackmailer. That conclusion spelled only one thing, Lauren was in far more danger than she knew.

I walked briskly back to Brock's office. When I got to his door, it was locked, and his classes schedule posted on the door clearly showed he had no classes to teach for the remainder of the day.

"Well," I said to myself, "the more you think, the harder it gets, so you better quit thinking and act!"

The first thing to do was to speak to Lauren as quickly as possible because as impossible as it seemed, I was convinced Brock was a physical threat to his sister and I needed to warn her of the danger he clearly represented.

The attractive Miss Swalia had dovetailed all the stray strands of the web to one inevitable conclusion. Lauren's brother Brock was certainly her blackmailer, and though I hadn't direct proof of the final strand yet, all the circumstantial evidence clearly implicated him as the killer in Timons death as well. It was the sole conclusion that had formed in the recesses of my limited imagination after Miss Swalia's mentoring. And maybe more so given her brother's current state of mental arousal due to his recent inspiration from Sister Aimee's apostatizing and the perceived threat his sister's misadventures with Timons would have on his family based on his over developed concept of right and wrong. The idea only grew stronger when I hadn't found the born-again professor in his office.

I headed full-tilt down the stairs to the first floor where I had seen a telephone booth. I slid into the booth and dropped a nickel into the slot, got a dial tone and dialed 7-0515, hoping to catch Lauren. Leaning against the glass, I considered how the differing strands of clues had now formed a perfect web.

First, Brock had proven with his fanatical diatribe in his office he was lacking in the most even of dispositions and was quite possibly mentally unstable. Second, his questionable temperament had shown itself years earlier during the sibling's collegiate years with Brock's assault on the young black musician and Lauren. There hadn't been a real relationship between the two siblings since. Thirdly, Timons had been dead less than twelve hours when his body was found in the lake and that Lauren had been the last person to see him alive, suggesting that one or possible both of them had been followed to their rendezvous.

This fact the sheriff's office had yet to learn. Only Lauren, I and the killer knew. Fourthly, the murderer and blackmailer both seemed to be someone close to Lauren, making it personal. Revenge seemed the more likely motive than the pursuant of financial gain. Fifth, though Brock hadn't spoken of it in his excited monologue. I believed he possessed racial hatred. And finally, and the most disconcerting of which, was the apparent impact Sister Aimee's apostatizing had had on Brock's belief system. The professor seemed convinced he was actually aiding mankind in rebuilding his vision of a moral America.

She didn't pick up, but remembering she had mentioned at lunch on Thursday that she used Sieber's Beauty Parlor. I put another nickel in the phone, got a dial tone, dialed the 0 and said, "Operator, please give me Sieber's Beauty Parlor."

I waited as the operator laughed. I hoped Lauren like most women told her hairdresser of forthcoming social plans. I was soon speaking to Mable at the beauty parlor. I quickly identified myself as a friend of Mrs. Camp's and was looking to speak to her. She stated she wasn't in the parlor at the moment, so I asked her who usually did Mrs. Camp's hair.

She hesitated for a moment before telling me the girl's name. "That would be Ronnie."

In a calm voice I inquired, "Could I speak to her for a moment?" She placed the receiver down and I waited for Ronnie to pick up.

A young sounding voice breathed into the phone. "This is Ronnie."

I introduced myself and told her I was supposed to meet Mrs. Camp at the shop to pick her up after her appointment, but that I was running late and needed to tell her to wait.

She spilled back, "You must have confused her instructions, Mr. Nayland. She doesn't have an appointment today. She told me she would be in the Deep Deuce today, providing condolences to friends of a family acquaintance that recently passed."

I thanked her and hung up the phone.

The case was breaking faster than I had expected, faster than I could handle by myself.

I found the sheriff's office phone number in my note pad. Put in my last nickel and dialed. It rang six times before I heard the baritone voice of the desk sergeant bellow into the receiver, "Sheriff's office."

"I need to speak to Sheriff Jackson," I almost yelled.

"Can I tell him who this is?" he said with skepticism.

"This is Lou Nayland, and I have some information he's been looking for," I said, exaggerating the truth.

"Hold on, I'll see if he'll take your call," the sergeant said into the mouthpiece.

Jackson's stern voice came on the horn. "What the hell you pulling, Nayland?"

In an excited and hurried tone, I told him. "It's the Camp matter. I think I know who killed the skin tickler and I can give you the red points to prove it. But time is short and the suspect may be heading to Deep Deuce as we speak to confront the Camp woman."

"Shit," he exclaimed.

"I prefer you come alone, I'm hoping we can handle this without you, or your boys, shooting up the whole community. I'll meet you at the corner of Second and Central in thirty minutes." I hung up the horn and stepped out of the phone booth, wiping the sweat from my puss with a damp handkerchief. Then I sprinted across campus to my car.

Chapter Twenty-Nine

I drove fast; always, when I find myself perturbed, I seek consolation in speed. The coupe hit nothing but the high spots on old U.S. 77 as the growing strands of clues crashed down through my churning cerebral matter. A few miles south of downtown, I slowed as I passed a state trooper parked along the highway. The cruiser contained two uniformed men looking grim. I checked my speedometer, nodded, and looked for the exit onto Fourth Street.

I turned the little coupe and pointed her west towards the Deuce as I tried to fit the missing pieces of the Camp puzzle together. The various slices turning over behind my eyes like a many-headed monster struggling to be born out of my mind. I turned onto Stiles and parked in front of Robinson's Drugstore. By this time I was certain that Brock was the missing piece.

I walked around the corner onto Second Street. Where I immediately I noticed a small crowd of locals forming in front of Hayward's Billiard's Hall. I saw Lauren standing in the middle of the street with both hands upon her hips, facing the Aldridge Theater. As I quickened my pace and came upon the outside of the crowd, I could clearly see her brother Brock standing under the Theaters marquee pointing his finger at Lauren.

I crossed the street and merged into the crowd closest to the Aldridge. Working my way forward to get closer to Brock, I suddenly bumped into Cecelia standing at the front of the crowd, absorbing the sparring sibling's verbal exchange. I wiggled up next to her, slightly touched her soft exposed shoulder. She startled as she turned towards me with fire in her eyes. I put a single finger to my lips, hoping she wouldn't respond. She just winked as we both turned our attention back to the siblings as their verbal tones intensified.

"Lauren, don't you realize your current behavior is evil and destroying your marriage and your soul?"

"You know nothing of Lesley and you're just a small, bigoted man."

Before he could retort, I yelled to Brock from the curb of the street, "I know Lesley Timons made trouble for you, and it appeared he was in a position to make more trouble for your sister and the family. You decided to put an end to that possibility. So I gather you lured him to a time and place of your own making with the possibility of payment of money."

I was guessing at some of it, but continued hoping Jackson would show up as I attempted to keep Brock engaged. "I assume Timons agreed to meet you, and when he did, you shot him and dumped his body at the lake."

He stood in the street shaking with angry as I finished. "Is that the way it happened, Brock?"

He wailed out, whirled in my direction and yelled, "That's a sinister little habit of yours, Mr. Nayland, asking personal questions of good people in the most public of places, and you seemed to have a perpetual case of it."

"Small, creepy murdering liars bring it out in me!" I retorted. "He was a human being. And somebody has to pay for his death!"

He took in my meaning slowly. Then it hit him like a slow motion bullet, disorganizing his face. "All right, gumshoe," he yelled at me and the growing crowd lining the street.

"I admit it, I killed Lauren's immoral drummer friend. But he had it coming for defiling my sister, publicly humiliating my family and conducting his life wickedly in every way. Besides, the up-standing members of this country couldn't care less if there is one less jazz musician in the world. Their music just contributes to the moral decay of God-fearing Americans." Brock was getting more worked up. "He was just a musician, a damn backslider. He produced nothing of value and did nothing that was in the furtherance of the founding faith. He only brought barbarism and heathenism into our great country."

The words fell from his lips along with several shots of spittle, as Lauren screamed, "How could you? You're the absolute devil!"

Her breath was quick and loud. "Lesley was a beautiful man and brilliant musician who only brought beauty into this world."

As I listened, I suddenly realized Cecelia had gone back into the Aldridge.

Brock started walking further into the street, closing the ground between him and Lauren. "I had to save you!" He shouted at her.

"Can't you understand? You had lost your way and you wouldn't listen to reason. I had to save you from yourself, before your soul was unredeemable before the Lord. You must understand! Everything I've done is for you."

While he begged his sister for understanding, I noticed that Sheriff Jackson, wearing street clothes, had come walking up from Central. He worked his way into the crowd behind Brock on the sidewalk. I thought one of us needed to make a move, but how to do it quietly, and with minimum harm to the pedestrians, was the question.

Lauren stood in the street with tears running down her freckled face. She cried out, "Why! Why! Why? Lesley was no threat to me, or my husband. He knew everything I did, and he enjoyed it in his own way. You know nothing, Brother." She let out a yelp of fury. "You're just a fool, a pious fool." She exclaimed as she fell to her knees onto the searing pavement, sobbing. Her body shook as she continued. "You're just an obsessed fanatic that has destroyed everything."

Brock walked to where Lauren sat crumpled on the street and pulled a cheap .32 auto, identical to the one I had seen in Lauren's purse, its nickel plating worn and corroded from inside his waistband and pointed it at her.

He yelled back, "You just don't get it. I have to save your soul. And divine guidance demands to do so I must kill you just like I killed your lover to wash the immorality from my own family. It's the first step in me achieving my destiny to cleanse this nation of its evil sinners and backsliders."

He raised both arms up over his shoulders declaring, "I can't become what I was born to be without first cleaning the immorality within my own house first, I'm truly sorry and I do love you, but I must." As the words escaped his lips, the sound of a gun shot bounced off the side of buildings bordering the street.

With the sound still ringing in my ears, I saw Brock's face open suddenly, eyes and mouth, as if he had wakened out of a nightmare. As I watched, I moved towards Lauren. She was unharmed. She sat shocked and staring back at her brother as he began to swaying to-and-fro, clutching his chest. As we all looked on, his legs buckled and he crumpled onto the hard surface of the street and rolled onto his side.

My eyes darted around the crowd. The reality of it all crashed down on me. Cecelia was standing outside the door of the Aldridge with a smoking S&W .38 in her hand. She looked as if it somehow had forced its way into her fist. She dropped it on the sidewalk as I headed towards her. As I did, two more shots rang out and Cecelia fell to the pavement. Two of those half-inch Colt slugs from Jackson's revolver caught her squarely in the chest.

I ran toward her. The smell of cordite drifted through the crowd as I knelt down next to her slumped body. She was still alive. I placed my left hand on the more serious of bullet wounds and pressed down in an attempt to stop the bleeding. Her large brown eyes were filled with tears as she tried to speak, a red froth bubbled from her lips. Her eyes began to glaze as she spoke. "He killed the only man I ever loved, Lou. He's evil. He had to be stopped. He had to pay for killing my beautiful Lesley."

Her nostrils dilated, and she paled. She caught a whiff of the fatal cordite. "You know I had to kill him. I couldn't let him live in a world where Lesley no longer existed. He didn't deserve to breathe another breath after he had destroyed such beauty." The final words escaped her lips along with the last breath from her lungs. I heard a whispered voice in the crowd, "That poor girl's dead!" I stood up. When I looked down, I saw a pool of blood forming on the sidewalk. The palm of my hand was sticky. All at once I felt sick in the pit of my stomach. I realized I had been scared as the shooting occurred. So scared, in fact, the backs of my knees were now aching.

Brice Jackson plodded over to the stage of this little drama with his service revolver still in his right hand. I sat holding Cecelia as I looked up at him. "Did you have to shoot her twice, Sheriff?"

"Maybe not, but she wasn't much use to herself alive. You might say that I saved her a lot of grief." He stated boldly as he re-holstered his wheel gun and said, "I think she had it all, all the grief there is honestly."

I sighed. "Maybe so. Either way, it's over for her now."

George exited the Aldridge Theater, walked to where I was holding Cecelia, took my place and wrapped his large arms around her now serene body.

I turned to face Brice and quietly asked, "I thought you were fond of the girl."

He stated flatly, "I was, that's why I finished it. We have the electric chair in this state. I've seen it in action. She was too beautiful of a soul to endure a trial, and a stay on the row awaiting a rendezvous with the chair. It was cleaner for her this way." Then, as if he had been reading my mind, he finished with, "She shouldn't have shot Brock. It was for the law to handle."

I stood there on the pavement looking at the destruction of human life, all brought about by a single act of love and thought. "Nothing in life ends 'right.'" As I continued pondering this sad fact, I looked back to Lauren holding her dying brother in her arms. I trudged back to the pair in the middle of the street.

A prowler car rounded the corner and squealed to a stop behind the crowd in the street. Two uniform city cops with outraged faces got out. One of the officer's had a sergeant's chevrons on his sleeve. He stared at the death before him. Brice sighed, stood back to let me pass him as I walked out to where Lauren was holding Brock. As I did so, he turned around and walked over to meet the city boys flashing his badge. I heard one of the cops, the sergeant, ask, "You handling this one, Sheriff?"

Brice barked to the officer without stripes. "There's a phone inside the Aldridge, call your headquarters. Get someone down with some clout, first. Then a meat-wagon." The patrolman rushed to the doors and slipped in for his search for the telephone.

Brock lay dying among the growing crowd there on Second Avenue. And as he did so, he looked up at his sister and spoke to her as she gently cradled him in her arms. Lauren's face grew soft as the corners of her mouth turned up into a bright smile. She looked remarkably young and virginal. The faint blue hallows under her eyes were dewy. Brock looked up into them. "I'm sorry I killed your friend. I followed an angel down the wrong path and lost myself along the way."

For a second I thought that Lauren the cool, Lauren the self-possessed, was going to fall forward in a dead faint. The blood drained out of her face, leaving her rich tan an unhealthy gray, and she wavered a moment before I put out a hand to steady her. She quickly recovered and drew her long soft fingers through her brother's hair, pulling them away from his now dimming eyes, smiling into them and sobbed in a low voice. "It doesn't matter now, really, does it? You just rest here in the sun and we'll wait here together for the doctor."

She pulled his head into her bosom for a long, drawn-out moment. The burning Oklahoma sun caused her silk blouse to soak through as the two of them sat there on the street. Brock pulled away and looked up into her eyes as he spoke,

"Man appears on earth for a little while; but of what went
before this life or of what follows, we know nothing."
                    Saint Bede

The words slipped from his dying lips as Lauren held his head in her hands. The brightly colored blood seeped from the corner of his mouth. The professor was dead.

Epilogue

After the Camp matter came to its grotesque conclusion on the streets of Deep Deuce, I had the balance of the week to look into the mystery baby question for my landlady's sister.

Since Mrs. Giannasi and her sister Menga were both Italian Catholics, I started my inquiries by attending a fundraising luncheon hosted by Catholic Daughters of America at St. Joseph's Cathedral on Fourth Street. I enjoyed a nice, baked macaroni and cheese lunch as I gathered as much gossip from this chicken house full of rumor-mongers.

Unfortunately, most of it was just idle gossip regarding the young Irish priest and the songs being sung by the choir. When I mentioned my landlady's sister, there was a rush by the gaggle to provide me with a few tidbits. The most important of which was the name of the young Brown's department store clerk named Carla Stover. She had left her position suddenly without a word to anyone, stirring up gossip in certain circles. These women believed unwed mothers tended to leave in the dead of night to avoid public scandal.

After I finished my lunch and excused myself from the gaggle, I drove out to Bethany, where the city's orphanage and the Nazarene Rescue Home for Unwed Mothers were run by Miss Mattie Malley. My investigation almost ended there when Miss Malley told me Miss Stover had been there when she delivered her daughter, but had since returned to her parents' farm out west in Hooker, Oklahoma.

I drove back to the Hightower to use my office phone. It just so happened that the local Postmaster in Hooker was a distant cousin, Virginia Cantrell.

As I dialed the number I noticed the front page of the *Daily Oklahoman* lying on my desk. The headlines read *Will Rogers Dies in Plane Crash*. I stopped dialing and picked up the paper and read the story.

August 15, 1935, Will Rogers, one of the most beloved American celebrities of our time, has died at the age of 55 in a plane crash in Point Barrow, Alaska, along with the plane's pilot, famous aviator, Wiley Post.

 Will Rogers, born in 1879 in now what is Oklahoma, began his career as a cowboy. But in his twenties, he moved on to life in the public eye as a vaudeville performer, showing crowds his skill with the lariat and his trademark humor....

I laid the paper back on my desk and redialed the number to Hooker. My cousin picked up the receiver on the first ring. I told her the young lady's name and asked if she knew anything about her current circumstances. In a sorrowful voice she informed me that the girl's new daughter had succumbed to 'dust pneumonia' in the last Black Roller earlier that month. We spoke briefly about connected family members, and then I thanked her and wished her family well.

On Monday I took Irene out to Holland Field for the Indians' third game of the pennant playoffs against the Beaumont Exporters. The teams entered the game tied 1-1 in the series. The Tribesmen won the game in the ninth inning with a home run. This marked their 103rd and gave them their first place finish and only Pennant title in their stint in the Texas League. I put my arm around Irene as we left the stadium and headed to her place for a much-needed night of relaxation and ecstasy I recalled a favorite quote of mine:

"Love is the most important thing in the world, but baseball is pretty good, too!"

      Yogi Berra

Acknowledgements

Thanks to Jeannie, Michelle and Justin for their input and encouragement.

About the Author

Scott Hartshorn is an attorney by training and has degrees in history, politics and the law. He has been a prosecutor and criminal defense attorney for 30 years. He and his wife Anne have been married for 33 years and have two children. Scott is a member of Mystery Writers of America, The Historical Novel Society, and of Sisters in Crime Writers Society.